NOTHING PINK

NOTHING PINK

Mark Hardy

FRONT STREET
Asheville, North Carolina

For Jim, and in memory of Carolyn and Skip Anderson

Copyright © 2008 by Mark Hardy
All rights reserved
Printed in the United States of America
Designed by Helen Robinson

LIBRARY OF CONGRESS CATALOGING-IN-PUBLICATION DATA
Hardy, Mark.
Nothing pink / Mark Hardy.—1st ed.
p. cm.
Summary: Vincent Harris, the teenaged son of a Baptist minister, has always
known he is gay and uses his faith to avoid any sinful thoughts or acts,
but when his family moves to a new church in the late 1970s he meets Robert Ingle,
falls in love, and begins to wonder if God is really asking him to repent and change.
ISBN 978-1-932425-24-6 (hardcover : alk. paper)
[1. Homosexuality—Fiction. 2. Christian life—Fiction. 3. Self-acceptance—Fiction.
4. Family life—Virginia—Fiction. 5. Virginia—Fiction.] I. Title.
PZ7.H221442Not 2008
[Fic]—dc22
2007017406

FRONT STREET
An Imprint of Boyds Mills Press, Inc.
815 Church Street
Honesdale, Pennsylvania 18431

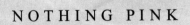

NOTHING PINK

CHAPTER ONE

My father begs people to come down to the altar, to get right with God.

Daddy doesn't need a microphone to be heard over our singing. "You're not keeping any secrets from God," he preaches. "It is God's Holy Spirit who, at this very moment, in this very room, reveals your sin to you."

Around me, stained-glass windows tell stories from the Bible. Jesus looks down with love on the ring of children sitting in a circle at His feet. His disciples serve loaves of bread and baskets of fishes. He walks on water. Sun shines through and casts tinted shadows all over the congregation. Nothing is its real color.

The bones in my fingertips are almost pushing through to the wood of the pew. Any second now, a nail will pop off, shoot across the sanctuary, and hit somebody upside the head. If I thought there was a snowball's chance in hell He'd really save me from sin this time, forever and ever amen, I'd pry my fingers off this pew and race down the aisle to that altar.

In front of me are rows and rows of pews. They're packed end to end with my father's new congregation, as packed as on Easter Sunday. Everybody, even the husbands, came to hear Daddy's first sermon, to check out God's new messenger. Maybe some of them came for the potluck immediately after the service. I can smell the food all the way in the sanctuary. It's nauseating.

I can't go down to the altar. Not on our first Sunday in this church. If people see their new preacher's son kneeling there, some of them will let their imaginations run wild, wondering what sin I've committed, why I'm on my knees. Other people will watch me sissy-walk down the aisle and notice that every hair is sprayed into place. It won't be hard for them to see how gay I am. They'll know right off what my sin is. I can't do that to my dad.

We sing verse two for the second time, "to rid my soul of one dark blot." We sing "Just as I Am" at almost every altar call. I could sing this song from memory way before I even knew what a dark blot was, much less that I had the darkest one. Since then I've made a zillion trips down to a million different altars and my blot hasn't gotten any lighter.

Some Sundays the Holy Spirit moves the way it did in the second chapter of Acts, like a mighty rushing wind, and the altar fills up fast, during the first few verses or so. Not today. Today people are waiting, wrestling with God. I used to be proud of myself for having the strength to step out into the aisle in front of the entire church and march down to the altar. I did it Sunday after Sunday. Today, I stand my ground and stay put in my pew.

I don't sing, but I mouth the words. *Fighting and fears, within, without.* Unless Daddy's head is bowed in prayer, he's looking out across the congregation. If he catches me not singing the hymn, I'll hear about it during Sunday dinner.

There are two reasons I don't sing. Number one: If I let any sound at all come out, my tear ducts will magically be activated and every man, woman, and child in my daddy's church will know what a big sinner their new preacher's son is. Number two: What's the point? I'm such a poor, wretched, blind sinner that singing won't help. If God was going to save me, He would have done it already on one of my zillion trips to the altar.

I don't need the hymnal for the words, so I return it to the rack. I only picked it up to hide my face. Both hands are free now, to hold on, to keep me here in this pew. At every pause, I breathe in deep, from my diaphragm, just like Mr. Elliott taught us in chorus. I don't need all this air for not-singing, but it sure eases my knuckle pain.

I mouth, *Oh, Lamb of God, I come. I come.*

I stay put, in my pew.

I made it through Daddy's sermon fine. And his prayers. I've trained myself to tune most of it out. But the singing always gets me crying, which makes it pretty obvious that God's calling me down to the altar. After that, there's no way I can stay in my pew. If I go, the congregation's got a preacher with a sinner for a son. If I don't go, they've got a preacher's son who doesn't follow the moving of the Holy Spirit.

At one end of the altar, an old lady picks up her cane. She pushes against it, up on one knee first, and then she stands. She's done her business with God. She limps back to her seat. Her tears haven't dried yet. Her eyes are still red and her face blotched, as if she caked today's powder and rouge on top of yesterday's. A handkerchief is tucked into the sleeve of her sweater. Only a little tongue of the hanky hangs out. She should take it and use it to wipe the tears that are two steps away from dripping on the carpet.

A boy in Momma's row gets up and heads for the altar. He can't be more than six. Isn't he too young to sin?

This morning Momma must have thought she was doing me some huge favor when she told me I didn't have to sit with her in the second row. She said it like she was releasing me from a prison sentence of life without parole. I could sit with the other teenagers "if I wanted to," she said, but I knew I didn't have a choice, so here I sit in the back row with all of them. Now only two people separate me from the boy in Sunday school who hissed like Satan every time I read a word with the letter *S* in it.

If I followed the Lord's leading, I'd have to sidestep across him and the other teens to get to the aisle. No matter how hard I squeezed against the pew, I wouldn't make it all the way without rubbing up against somebody. Too much could go wrong.

Momma leans back, lets another old lady by. Momma's singing without her hymnal. From behind, I can see her head barely nod as her mouth changes with the words. I strain my ears and try to hear her above the rest of the congregation. That voice always fills our house.

I don't think Momma had to wonder why I used to go down to the altar so often. She must have known I'm gay. Now that I'm staying in my pew she thinks I'm healed, but she can't see into my soul. She can't feel what's always there at the center of every single solitary cell in my body.

We learned about cells in Life Science. Mitosis and meiosis. Mitochondria. Cytoplasm. If I were a single cell, homosexuality would be my nucleus.

If I go down now, Momma will think I backslid. That while she's been job hunting, I've been sneaking off with some new neighbor boy doing Sodom-and-Gomorrah things.

Mr. Herndon, my new Sunday school teacher, kneels at the altar. His head is bowed so low he looks headless. Even without his head, he's taller than the other kneeling, praying people. The soles of his shoes are barely scuffed. A silver thumbtack is stuck in one heel. Jerry Duff put a thumbtack like that in my chair during the Pledge of Allegiance once. After sitting down on it, I never let on that the thumbtack was sticking through my pants into my leg. When Mrs. Dillard called my name and I stood up to get in line for lunch, there was blood. I had to tug to get the thumbtack out. All I cared about was not letting anyone see me do it. They'd all know why Jerry Duff chose me.

Mr. Herndon leans his elbows on the altar, folds his hands in prayer. His coattail splits into an upside-down V. I can't tell if he's crying. Even if he is, it's not proof his tears are shed for his own sins. Some nights I peek through the crack in Momma's door and watch her kneeling by her bed praying and crying. Over me, I'm sure. Daddy is always asleep, snoring.

Earlier in the service, after Daddy read the scripture but before he started to preach his sermon with a not-very-funny joke, he made Momma and me stand up and turn around so everybody could get a good look at us. He introduced us like that man who announces this week's contestants on *The Dating Game.*

Daddy wasn't done with that introduction before half the congregation could tell about me. My hair is a dead giveaway. People sometimes think I'm a girl because of my feathered Farrah Fawcett hairdo, but I just can't cut my hair off. They can see the queer in every layer of hairspray. I see it, too, but I can't quit spraying Aqua Net.

It's not really the hairspray, I know. John Travolta wears hairspray—he practically invented the whole feathered look—but nobody on earth thinks he's gay. Bruce Jenner won a bunch of gold medals, and his hair is more perfect than John Travolta's could ever hope to be. But who'd call him a faggot? He wins decathlons. He won eight gold medals. He's on the cover of the Wheaties box.

Daddy pinches the bridge of his nose between his thumb and pointer finger. His glasses lift above his eyebrows. He carries his Bible with him and paces silently behind the altar, listens, for what seems like eternity before stopping dead in his tracks. He's heard God's voice.

"Just as I Am" is a soft hymn; he doesn't have to speak very loud. He takes his glasses off and puts them in his coat pocket. "I'm going to ask Miss Macy to continue playing softly," he tells the congregation.

The altar fills up and runs over. A few people have to use the front pew as their altar and kneel there.

The congregation can tell he's not done talking. Their

singing trickles off. Daddy crosses the front of the sanctuary, stops at the far end of the altar.

He goes on, "I'm going to ask each of you to bow your head in silence. To close your eyes and wait while the Lord speaks."

The Lord (I'm pretty sure it's Him) doesn't leave me long in my silence. "Go," He says.

I always go. And the new heart He gives me hardly makes it back to the parsonage. Lately, I'm lucky if I don't back-slide before dessert. I look at the brass cross on the altar or at the baptismal pool behind it, where sinners are dunked in the name of the Father and the Son and the Holy Ghost. I cannot turn my head Daddy's way. I stare down at the tile floor until I realize it's way too obvious that I'm trying to hide from God, so I look up, at the flower arrangement in front of the pulpit. I wait for God to speak again, but I doubt He will. Unless God speaks through my father, He is a man of few words.

These flowers are from a florist, not grown in the gardens of the old church ladies like the ones back at Mount Hermon Baptist. Old ladies don't grow carnations; they grow roses. Daylilies and dahlias and buttercups. Tulips. Flowers that have a smell. Only florists use baby's breath and those fake-looking fern branches.

On each side of the flowers, there's a tall white candle in an even taller brass candlestick. I watch the flame on my left. They're not electric light-bulb candles, the fake kind you put in your windows at Christmas. They're real candles with real flames that leap up the way our souls leap up for God. I learned that in confirmation class when I was twelve. My soul has been leaping up for God as long as I can remember. I used to feel like I reached Him, but lately, I feel more like a Chihuahua than a flame—too short no matter how high I jump. God is always there, my Master, grinning down from above. He holds a juicy steak bone over my head. Holds it just out of reach. I jump and jump and jump, but every time I get anywhere near the bone, God jerks the string and the bone jumps higher. I remember the days when He was cutting my steak up into little pieces and feeding them to me. I want those days back.

Daddy kneels in front of Mr. Johnny, who's almost as tall kneeling as Daddy is standing up. He must be almost seven feet tall, because my daddy's not a short man. When I was a kid, I loved to watch Daddy work the altar like this. He comes off so holy that he looks like Jesus Himself, practically floats from sinner to sinner. Today is his first Sunday shepherding this congregation, but already you can see Daddy's love for his people, his sheep, all over his face as he prays with them, red-faced, straining, sweat pouring as he wrestles with the devil on their behalf and helps them pray through to victory. When they turn and walk up the aisle, you see God in their faces. You'd think Daddy had just given every last one of them a million dollars.

I don't want to see it anymore. I look back down at the tile floor instead, the same speckled linoleum tile that was in the locker room at Phelps Road Middle School. Except the Phelps Road tile was turquoise and this church tile is beige. I'm angry now, and I don't know why.

There's a piece of gravel on the floor; someone must have

tracked it in from the parking lot. I stretch out my leg, reach my foot under the pew in front of me, and step down hard on the sharp gray pebble. I can feel it through the thick leather sole of my Sunday shoe. An inch or two at a time, I pull my foot back. I hear the scrape over Miss Macy's soft playing. I look left and then right, over my shoulder. No one else seems to hear.

I inspect the damage. It makes no sense, but seeing the groove I cut in the tile softens the anger in me.

Miss Macy's not playing "Just as I Am" anymore. I never heard her switch songs. I can't tell what she's playing. I tune out Daddy and listen only to the piano. It's a slowed-down, soft version of "What a Mighty God We Serve." A song that usually gets people up on their feet, clapping and shaking tambourines, waving fans, marching in the aisles.

Behind closed lips, I sing to the beige tile. *What a mighty God we serve. What a mighty God we serve.* But not mighty enough to fix me. Or just not willing, which is worse.

I admire the rut I dug with the gravel. But it's not enough: not deep enough or long enough. With the toe of my shoe, I move the gravel back to its starting point. I step down harder this time, and again I pull my foot back inch by inch, carving deep into the tile. I pull the gravel back, farther and farther, until my leg is bent under the pew, as far as it can go. I move my foot away and check out my work again. My rut is now a gully. At one end, a sliver of linoleum is curled up like a pig's tail.

I've never so much as held hands with a boy under a blanket at a football game. I've never kissed a boy behind my open locker door, or slow-danced to a Commodores song at a sweetheart dance. I've never lied to my teacher and said I had to go to the bathroom and instead slipped a love letter through the slots in another boy's locker. So why am I going to hell? If I go down to the altar, what do I repent?

Is it evil to walk and talk like a girl? There's not one word in the Bible about the sin of fumbling a football. There's no Thou shalt not spend Saturday night helping your mom curl her hair up on sponge rollers while the cake you just made from scratch fills the house up with air so chocolaty it covers the beauty-shop stink of home-permanent solution.

Since the day my babysitter Miss Eloise caught me with the men's underwear section of her Sears catalogue, I haven't let more than a few lustful thoughts hang around in my mind. And I knelt down beside my bed a long time ago to confess them before God. I chase those thoughts away with memorized scripture verses, and when that doesn't work, I hum hymns until every lustful picture is out of my mind. The second a dream turns sexy, I wake myself up. When *The Wild Wild West* comes on—or *Three's Company* or *Mork & Mindy* or *Emergency!*—I flip the channel. Those men in tight pants can be too much.

One day in the locker room I heard Jay Crider tell Ken Craddock exactly how you do it, but I still don't, to use God's words, "spill my seed out onto the rock." Sometimes when I'm asleep it spills out on its own, but I can't help that. Besides, it's not a sin if it's not on purpose, if you don't choose to do it.

I've never committed a single sinful act with a boy, but I know if God doesn't save me, if I die before he rips the queer demons out by their roots, I'm going to burn in hell for eternity.

I know all this. But so far not one of my trips to the altar has changed me. If I thought God would stiffen my wrists, lower my voice, and make it the ladies' lingerie section of the Sears catalogue I need to steer clear of, I'd go down there again.

Daddy finishes praying with another elderly lady. The senior citizens in this church sure are sinful. He cups his hand around the crown of her head and kisses her between the eyebrows. I wonder if her husband minds. I imagine Daddy with long hair and a beard, a long white robe. Looking like Jesus, washing His disciples' feet.

Daddy stands up and sidesteps to the next person. Before he kneels again, he says to us, "The Lord tells me there are others who need to come." How can he be so sure he's hearing God's voice when I'm always afraid the voice I hear is Satan in disguise?

He preaches to me, calls me to the altar. I don't go. I don't look him in the eye. Daddy preaches at the top of his lungs and God is silent.

"God says if you take a single step of faith, just one step out into that aisle, His divine angels will meet you there and carry you the rest of the way on their wings."

A man coughs and a few seconds later the crinkle of a peppermint being unwrapped echoes through the sanctuary. Other people cough, quieter than the first man. I barely hear them unwrap their mints.

Daddy pauses between kneeling sinners. He looks out over the congregation, moves his head like a submarine periscope. "There's healing in His hands. Won't you come?"

I've heard him say these exact words a million times.

Save me, Lord. Please, save me. I've prayed it for as long as I can remember. I used to mean it more. I used to scream this to myself in the mirror when Momma and Daddy weren't home. Over and over and over. This morning I can barely mumble the complete sentence under my breath. My soul's not in it anymore. It's barely got the energy to get itself out of bed in the morning, let alone to leap for God. Asking Him to turn me into a non-queer feels just like asking Momma if I can stay up late to watch *Saturday Night Live*. Why bother if the answer is always no?

I've read the Bible cover to cover three times. I've sat in church and listened to more sermons than probably any other fourteen-year-old on Planet Earth. Then gone home and stayed up half the night staring at the ceiling, playing back those sermons in my mind. Over and over again.

I've heard Daddy preach it and preach it. I know if I die with one single unconfessed sin in my heart I will go straight to the fiery pit of hell. Just like the Chance card says, I will not pass Go, I will not collect two hundred dollars.

I don't want to go to hell, but the sad thing is, nothing that my daddy or any other preacher on the face of this earth has said or done can keep me out.

From the corner of my eye, I watch Daddy. He kneels and prays with one sinner, stands, kneels, then prays with the next. Sinner by sinner, he makes his way across the altar. He touches each sinner somewhere: hand, shoulder, elbow, neck. Kisses the women between the eyebrows before they turn away and he sidesteps to the next kneeling sinner.

I pick the pig's tail up off the floor. I roll it between my thumb and pointer finger. I try to shape the curl into a perfect sphere, but the brittle lineoleum crushes, crumbles between my fingers. The crumbs fall to the floor. I roll and roll. The friction heats my fingertips. The last crumb drops to the floor. Dust.

I curl my hand and bow my head. I don't go. I don't cry. I'm not even fighting tears, not a one. I'm all dried up. My eyes are wide and numb. My hands relax, resting on the pew in front of me. The blood has flooded back under my fingernails.

CHAPTER TWO

At the potluck, Momma and Daddy and I were whisked off to the front of the line. We're supposed to be filling our plates and making our way down the long table, but people keep breaking in, shaking hands with my father, telling him what a great sermon he preached, how blessed Bethlehem Baptist is to have him as their minister.

A tall boy crosses the fellowship hall. I try to look at the people talking to my father, but I turn away to watch this boy. I think he's heading for the dessert table, but he comes over to us. I don't recognize him from Sunday school. He stands behind the altar-call lady who had the hanky sticking out of her sleeve, with his hands folded in front of him. When she says, "God bless you," and steps away, he moves in for his turn.

"I'm Robert Ingle," he says. Wrist cocked, ladylike, he offers his hand to me. Not to my father or my mother, as everyone else has done. To me.

His nails are long and buffed, if not actually coated in clear polish. Someone did a fine job starching his shirt collar. Every hair is in place, like John Travolta's. I wonder if he uses Aqua Net. There are a few dots of dried blood on his neck from where he shaved this morning. A five o'clock shadow is already showing, even though it can't be later than one o'clock. I take his hand. It is cool and smooth, like Momma's.

"I'm Vincent," I say. Then add, "Vincent Harris." I can't believe I took his hand, let alone talked to him.

"I know," he says. "I'm Robert." Then blushes to realize he just repeated himself. "Want to sit with us?"

Robert Ingle turns—not just his head, but his entire top half—toward the teens' table. They are watching. As we let go of our handshake, he gently squeezes my fingertips just before we completely separate. My hand tingles. I rub a finger back and forth under my nose, pretend it itches. The smell of Jovan Musk for Men is unmistakable.

I study the teenagers at Robert Ingle's table. There is an empty chair in front of the picked-over plate of food he abandoned to come invite me. The one beside it is the only other chair empty. If I turn him down, the teens will think the new preacher's son is a snob. Even so, sitting with Momma and Daddy will be safer. If I'm halfway across the fellowship hall, the teenagers won't be able to hear the homo in my voice.

A painting of Christ hangs over their heads. His palms are pierced. A few drops of blood, shaped like perfect tears, drip from each hand.

Robert Ingle doesn't wait for my answer. "I saved you a seat next to me."

Back home, in the basement, I pull the ottoman up as close as I can get it to the TV. Underneath the thin linoleum is cement, so cold it keeps the floor freezing, even during summer. Sometimes, on really hot days, I take off all my clothes and stretch out naked on the floor and flip from my back to my stomach, over and over.

Now I pull my feet up, sit cross-legged. I touch my nose to the screen and watch the movie. There's no one here to tell me I'll go blind.

I'm allowed only two hours of television a day. If I can keep Momma and Daddy from knowing I'm watching *Paper Moon* right now, I'll still have both my hours to watch TV after church tonight.

My ear is inches from the speaker. I can feel the words against my skin. I can't turn the sound down any lower or get any closer. My hand is on the volume dial, ready to switch the TV off in a split second if my parents wake up and I hear their footsteps coming down the hallway.

When I asked to be excused from the table and told them I was going downstairs to take a nap, it wasn't a lie. I hadn't planned to watch TV. I undressed for a nap, stripped down to just socks and underwear, and lay on my bottom bunk, but I couldn't fall asleep. I used my big toes to pull off both socks. I counted the number of water spots on the cinder-block walls. No matter what I did, I couldn't get my mind off the boy from the potluck dinner.

Now I'm watching television, but my mind is still on Robert Ingle. It plays like a broken record, stuck on his seersucker suit, on how at the same time he both towered over me and looked me square in the eye. I inhale hard and try to bring back the smell of his musk.

The little girl in the movie, who has a boy's haircut, sleeps with her head in her daddy's lap. Before I started kindergarten, I used to ride this way with my father, when we'd drive to preach revival meetings in other towns. I still go with him during the summer. I just quit falling asleep on his shoulder.

The telephone rings. I don't know how I know, but I know it's him. Before the second ring I'm on my feet and halfway across the den, almost to the telephone. I tiptoe as if I'm walking on a bed of hot coals. My feet barely touch the floor long enough to feel the cold cement through the linoleum.

I pick up the receiver, but Momma's already talking on the other phone. I squeeze the earpiece between my ear and shoulder and cover the mouthpiece with the palm of my hand.

"Marnni Harris speaking." Momma always answers the phone with the words "Bethlehem Baptist parsonage," or whatever church's parsonage we're living in. She must have already gotten out that part. She's so perky it's impossible to tell she's been woken up in the middle of a nap.

I imagine Momma lying there before the phone rang, in her and Daddy's bed, still in her Sunday best, all neatly laid out, careful not to wrinkle. Her shoes are tucked under the bed, side by side, her pantyhose balled up and stuffed in one shoe. She looks like a corpse except that she has her eyeglasses folded in the middle of her chest where a lily would be.

"This is Robert Ingle, ma'am. I go to Bethlehem Baptist." Before he finishes his sentence, I am feeling his lotioned handshake, hearing those too-soft *S*'s.

I run my finger along one of the grooves in the wood

paneling. I picture him as he was when we shook hands—starched collar, perfect hair, towering above me. The baby-blue stripes in his suit made him look even taller.

The sound of his voice slows my breath down. I've read about this feeling, but I've never had it before. Is this what girls feel when they come out of the bathroom giggling about a boy? Is it this feeling that makes them cover their notebooks in hearts and his initials?

"I met you today." Robert squeaks out the last word. "At the potluck." His pitch gets higher. His sissy sound is the one I always try to cover up. It pumps fear into my throat. At church he didn't seem so gay.

It's my mother's turn to talk, but she doesn't say a word. Can she hear queer too?

Robert continues, "My parents said to make sure and tell you ..."

I worry about Momma hearing him speak a sentence with so many *S*'s, so I pull the phone down against my chest, breathe deep, and then raise it back to my ear. There is silence. I'm sad to think they've hung up, but there's no dial tone. I keep listening. Finally Robert says, "Is Vincent home? Your son, Vincent?"

This time, Momma leaves just a tiny pause. "I think he's taking a nap," she says. I feel her fear through the phone line. I hate it that she said *nap*. It makes me sound like such a baby.

Robert doesn't do the polite thing, the thing she wants him to do. He doesn't say, *I'll call back later*, or *Can I leave him a message?* He waits Momma out, until she says, "Why don't I run check?"

I hear their bedroom door shut behind her, hear her bare feet march down the hallway toward the top of the stairs.

I hold my palm over the mouthpiece. She must have laid her phone on the bedside table because in the background I can hear Daddy humming "Amazing Grace." I hang up the phone with my finger and keep the button pressed down. I do not return the handpiece to its cradle; I just switch it to the other ear. Momma never comes all the way downstairs, so I stay put, but on alert, ready to bolt to my room any second.

"Vincent!" Momma calls from the top of the stairs. She thinks her voice has to travel all the way across the basement and through my bedroom door and wake me up from the nap I said I was taking. Twice as loud she yells, "Pho-o-o-one." When I don't answer that instant, she calls, "It's for you."

I count to twenty and then yell, "I've got it, Momma." I let my finger off the button I've been holding down.

"This is Vincent," I say in my most businesslike voice into the phone.

Momma thumps back down the hallway. Their bedroom door closes behind her. I stop hearing Daddy hum. She must have hung up the receiver in their room.

My toes are starting to go numb, as if I've been playing in the snow. I move one foot on top of the other. The cold sole of my left foot shocks the top of my right.

"This is Robert, Robert Ingle. From church."

I know that. I give him a dose of Momma's silent treatment.

Robert fills the silence. "You didn't sit with me."

I hear disappointment in his voice, not anger. I am ready

to blame it on Momma if he asks why I didn't sit at his table. But he doesn't, so finally I say, "What's up?"

"Want to come over?" He doesn't sound like his mother put him up to it.

"Right now?" I pull the phone back away from my ear.

"Now or later. Whenever. My mom says I can pick you up in her car."

"I can't right now," I say. "I've got to get ready for church." I speak before I remember that it's only two-thirty. That gives me four and a half hours to get ready for church.

If he catches the mistake, he doesn't call me on it. "Your father's starting a Sunday night service?"

"He always does." I'm sad to be off the subject of me coming over. "Will you be there?" I ask like I really want him to be, and I do. At least, part of me does. The other part of me knows it would be easier if Robert Ingle was a heathen who came to Sunday morning worship only.

I write my name in the dust on top of the phone, then blow my fingertip clean. A beam of sun pours through the tiny basement window. My telephone dust floats in this spotlight like dandelion fluff.

"I doubt it," he says. "My family watches *Wild Kingdom* and *Wonderful World of Disney* on Sunday night. It's a tradition. My sister drives up from Danville with her twins."

"What's that guy's name? Marlin Perkins?" I ask like I don't know for sure Marlin Perkins is the man on *Mutual of Omaha's Wild Kingdom*, but I do. Sometimes I fake being sick and Momma and I stay home to watch him.

"It's Marlin something," Robert confirms.

"You should come." As soon as the words are out of my mouth, I can't believe I said them. But as long as I said them, I might as well make sure he knows what I'm talking about, so I add, "To the Sunday night service."

As if he didn't hear me, he says, "What about after church? We could go for ice cream or pizza." He rattles this off so fast I get the impression he sat home thinking of ideas in advance.

Is he asking me out on a date? I pull the phone so close to my mouth that my lips touch plastic. I can't go to either of those places on Sunday. It's a sin to buy things on the Sabbath, to make people work on the Lord's Day.

Robert takes my silence for a no. "To a movie?"

His persistence doesn't turn me off. He isn't desperate or pitiful. I coil the phone cord around my finger, unwind, twist it around again. I see us there in the movie theater. Our hands bump into each other in a tub of buttered popcorn. We share a Coke, same straw.

And then I know. I will not go anywhere with Robert Ingle. Won't even be seen in public with him. I can never be his friend, let alone his boyfriend. It's a rule: *Flaming queers shall not be friends.*

It's bad enough with kids just thinking I'm gay. If I hang out with another known queer, I give them all the proof they need. There will be no end to our misery. Even if I never go farther than first base with him, people will picture us way past that. Everyone, including my mother. Especially Momma.

I walk toward the stairs, stretch the cord as far as it will go, straighten out its pig's-tail curves. I stop in the spotlight of sun.

"I'll have to ask my parents," I tell Robert, and I cover the mouthpiece with my hand again. The linoleum warms the soles of my feet. I stand in the sun and count to a thousand while Robert waits for me to ask my parents' permission.

After Robert's call, I start my grooming ritual extra-early—just in case he does come to church tonight. I'm soaking in a bubble bath when Momma knocks on the bathroom door. Until then, I'm positive I've gotten away with telling Robert she said no. But the bathroom is the one place she never bothers me.

"Can I come in?"

Maybe it's not what I'm thinking. Maybe she needs a towel, or forgot her makeup. If I had locked the door, I could use that as my excuse, but instead I say a weak "Okay."

She opens the door barely wide enough to step through and closes it behind her, like she's sneaking. "I only need a minute."

When I was a kid, after I played in the tub until I was a wrinkled prune, she would come in and wash me. But I out-grew that years ago.

My water has turned lukewarm. Most of the bubbles have popped. The soapy white mountain has thinned to a layer I can almost see my privates through. I swish my hands to stir up new suds.

She's carrying some magazine, her pointer finger marking a certain page. Maybe it's an ad for one of those camps for

Christian gays, where they brainwash homosexuality away. If I thought it would work, I'd sign myself up. But something just doesn't seem right about it—all those gay boys in one place.

Momma puts the toilet lid down and sits, crosses her legs. "I have a confession," she says quietly.

I rub the bar of Ivory soap around and around in the washcloth. The smell burns the inside of my nose.

"I listened to your phone call." She doesn't give me time to protest her violation of my privacy. "I heard you tell that boy Robert I wouldn't give you permission to go to his house this afternoon." When she uses her soft voice, I can never tell if she's angry or disappointed or both.

I sink in the tub until only my knees and neck and head remain out of the water. Now that my shoulders are immersed I realize how cold the air is and how chilly things are with my mother.

She puts the magazine down on the counter and picks up the dental floss. She tears off a long piece of it and wraps one end around each pointer finger, then watches herself wrap and wrap until the floss between her two fingers is the perfect length.

She's waiting for me to go next, to explain my lie. I pretend I don't know what she's talking about. I slide all the way under the water and hope she's gone when I come up for air.

She's not. She's done with her teeth, but she's not gone. The dental floss dangles from one finger. Momma inspects a gross piece of food, then unwinds the floss and drops it into the trashcan. She stands up and moves to the edge of the tub.

I hold my washcloth over my privates. She is too close. I

pinch my legs around my hand. A mother should never be this near her naked teenage son.

"You've got to call him back."

Momma hands me what I thought was a magazine but can now see is the Bethlehem Baptist Church phone directory. I don't take it from her. My hands are wet.

"Who?" I say. Still playing dumb. She watches me watch myself squeeze Prell shampoo into the palm of my hand.

"You can blame it on me, Vincent. Tell him your fickle mother changed her mind."

I quit squeezing the tube, which sucks air back in and farts. Momma's little laugh gives me permission to let out a little laugh of my own. "I didn't lie on purpose, Momma. I swear."

She doesn't look at me. She just waves the phone directory in front of my face, half joking, and places it on the closed toilet seat. "He's listed under Robert Ingle, Senior. Call him."

CHAPTER THREE

It's Tuesday. Just two short days since I called Robert.

As soon as I got out of the bathtub that night, I dialed him from the upstairs phone to make it easy for Momma to eavesdrop. I knew just what to suggest we could do. I've been taking care of our neighbor's horse, Happy, while his daughter is at Governor's School in Richmond. I invited Robert to help me feed and groom her today.

I wait for him in Daddy's parked car. He'll be here any second. I turn on the radio and tune the dial to K-92 FM, a brand-new station out of Roanoke. Barry Manilow is singing "Copacabana," which has been on Casey Kasem's *American Top 40* forever.

Daddy lets me crank the car when I'm listening to music so I won't kill the battery. The air conditioner is on so high that chill bumps cover my arms. Since we don't have a radio in the house, I'm out here often. Usually I roll the windows down and sweat it out, save Daddy's gas, but today I don't want to mess up my hair or stain my armpits.

Robert's due at two o'clock. When we're through grooming Happy, Momma says, we are to come back over to the parsonage for apple dumplings. She wants a long, close look at him.

Right now, Momma is sitting at the kitchen table circling Help Wanted ads in the *Danville Register and Bee*. She's looking for a secretarial job. A batch of her famous 7-Up apple dumplings is already in the oven. When I was blow-drying my hair, I smelled them baking from all the way down in the basement.

Daddy is in his study at the church. It would be just like him to watch Robert's arrival from between the slats of his venetian blinds. He spends hours every day locked in there with his Bible. I'm sure he has his own suspicions about me. He's probably praying for my lost soul this very moment. I hope not. If I'm lucky, God's got Daddy so wrapped up in writing Sunday's sermon he won't even hear Robert's car pull into the parking lot.

If I didn't know secular music was a sin and if Barry wasn't singing about a nightclub where people drink and dance, I'd swear God was here in the car, beside me in the passenger's seat. He harmonizes with Barry. He doesn't order me to switch the station to WVOG, the Voice of God for the People of God.

I watch for Robert through the windshield. I don't want him to sneak up on me and catch my dance. But Barry's music takes me away to the disco where Lola is a showgirl and jealous Rico who wears a diamond and Tony the bartender shoot each other over their love for her.

Poor Lola. Left to sit all alone in that dress she used to wear, the feathers in her hair all faded. I play drums on the steering wheel and sing about how Lola drank herself half blind and thought about Tony until she lost her mind.

I reach to turn the volume up higher, but it's already as loud as it will go. The bongos and Barry's voice are static-y.

Every inch of me from the waist up dances. The car ceiling is just above my head, so I can't stretch my arms very high. They writhe around each other, two cobras coming out of a basket. With my right foot, I tap out the rhythm on the gas pedal. The engine revs with each beat.

Suddenly the car bounces—a slow rock, like someone on a high dive getting up his nerve to jump. In the rearview mirror, Robert is mouthing words I can't make out. Where did he come from?

Every hair is in place, only it's parted on the side today, not straight down the middle. It bounces in rhythm with the motion of the car.

By the time I have my window rolled all the way down he's leaning against the driver's door with his arms crossed on the roof. I keep my eyes on him and turn the key off. Everything dies at once—the engine, the air conditioning, Barry's voice.

"How did you get here?" My throat is so scratchy from singing at the top of my lungs that I can barely squeeze out sound.

"I walked."

"You snuck up on me." Just how much of my act did he watch before he started bouncing the car?

Robert crosses his arms into an *I Dream of Jeannie* pose and leans down onto the windowsill. He rests his chin on his arms and looks right at me, holds the stare. Our faces are inches apart. His eyes are the same blue as mine. His hair is soap-opera perfect.

I say, "I thought you were driving your mom's car."

"I was, but my mom's hair appointment got changed, so I walked."

Now I see the sweat. Streams of it run down his forehead and are absorbed by his eyebrows. In the center of his chest, sweat has leaked through his T-shirt. I am surprised to find it sexy.

I expected him to show up in some preppy outfit with ironed creases and a starched Polo shirt collar standing straight up. Instead, he's wearing faded Levi's with a grass stain on the knee.

His T-shirt has been ironed, though. He sees me staring at the John Deere logo and says, "My dad got it when he bought his new tractor." He pulls at the silkscreened silhouette.

I take Daddy's keys out of the ignition. His Cross-in-My-Pocket keychain cuts into my hand. I pull the car door handle, Robert takes a step back, and I hop out. Earlier, the air was dead still, but now, standing less than a foot away from Robert, I can feel a breeze.

Robert starts dancing to music that no longer blares from the car stereo. He doesn't disco to the beat of "Copacabana" like they do on *American Bandstand*. Instead, he does a ballroom step. One hand is curved around the waist of an imaginary partner. He dances on his toes, twirls and dips. He could be on *The Lawrence Welk Show*.

Robert's tall enough to be on the basketball team. He's

not bony, the way I remember him. He's more cowboy than Broadway dancer. Malibu Barbie skin. I bet he greases up with Johnson's baby oil and iodine and lies out in the sun for hours.

Under the carport, the kitchen storm door swings open and Momma steps halfway out. She is about as far away from us as the back church pew is from the altar. She's wearing a yellow shirtdress the color of black-eyed Susans. It's the middle of summer and she has it buttoned to the top. Her dress is seersucker, like Robert's suit last Sunday.

She's holding a plastic gallon jug full of iced tea. Two Styrofoam cups are turned upside down on the jug's lid, like a hat.

Halfway out the door, halfway in, she watches Robert dance. She and Daddy don't believe in dancing, not even if moved by the Holy Spirit. Her muscles are tensed up like a stray dog that somebody is trying to take food from. Robert's back is to her. He doesn't feel her disapproval. He dances as if he has no idea dancing is a sin.

The apple-dumpling smell pours out of the open kitchen door.

"What kind of trouble are you boys planning on getting into?" Momma says. Joking, but not totally. Robert keeps his feet planted but still moves above the waist. He just can't quit.

Momma takes a step toward Robert. Sweet tea sloshes and ice rattles against the plastic. She must have crushed some ice to make it fit through the mouth of the milk jug. When I'm sick she wraps ice in a dishrag and pounds it with a hammer. Crushed ice is her cure for fever.

Momma's eyes catch sight of Robert's sneakers. He's wearing Chuck Taylors, real Chucks. She's probably noticing that he's not wearing socks, which surprises me too—not wearing socks is dirtier and smellier than I thought he'd let himself be. Momma hates shoes worn without socks. It's almost a sin to her.

Robert finally tunes in to Momma's glare and stops dancing altogether. "So, what are we doing this afternoon?" he asks.

"We're going over to Mr. Red Evans' barn." No one says anything, so I add, "Is that all right?" I'm not sure which of them I'm asking.

Momma shifts. Hands me the jug of tea and Robert the Styrofoam cups. She does an about-face. Halfway back to the kitchen, she calls over her shoulder, "You boys behave."

As we walk, an invisible magnet keeps pulling me into him. I say, "Excuse me," and he says, "No prob," like we are strangers bumping into each other on a busy city sidewalk. The third time I bump into him, I pull back and start to lag behind a step or two.

We walk through the church graveyard. Robert stops to point out his grandparents' graves. Both their names are on the same tombstone. First I notice that they both died the year I was born, 1965, and then I see that the date is exactly the same for both of them, August 4. When I turn back to him, he has unscrewed the cap off the gallon jug and is taking a swig of tea. I'm not thirsty—we've been walking for only a few minutes—but when he offers it to me I take the jug and drink from it anyway. There is no taste of his lips left behind.

A short stream of tea leaks out the corner of my mouth. I pull the jug away and pass it back, wipe my face with my hand. Robert takes another swig and screws on the plastic lid. I don't ask him to tell me the story of both grandparents dying on the same day. I don't want one ounce of sadness now.

Sprigs of grass are starting to grow on a fresh grave just a few plots ahead of us. Some tombstones have cement statues of lambs and angels on top; some are simple rectangles. On the few graves that have flowers, the flowers are faded. The plastic ones hold their color better than the silk ones.

Robert sees an arrangement that has blown over and sets it back upright. Normally I would help him tidy up the graveyard, but I'm not trying to make my best impression. It would be easier if he never wanted to do this again.

A few steps more and he picks up a stray lily, looks around, tries to match it with the right grave. He quits and puts the lily behind his ear.

I get to soak up the sight of Robert with the lily behind his ear for only a second. Then I'm hit with the fear that Daddy has been watching us through his study window, spying, and I want to take that plastic lily from behind Robert's ear and trample it under my foot. The rest of the walk, I stay a few steps behind him. The farther away from the church we get, the less the lily bothers me. By the time we are at Mr. Red's barn, I've caught back up to Robert.

Robert wipes his forehead with the cold jug of tea. He holds it a few seconds against each cheek, presses it hard into his skin. I'm used to seeing him with the lily behind his ear now. I don't want to trample it anymore.

Happy is on the far side of the pasture, grazing on grass. Her lead shank hangs just inside the barn door. I reach in and take it off its nail, hold it out to Robert. I want to watch him walk across the field. I want Happy to run from him, to be hard for him to catch. I want him to have to call me for help.

"You catch her." I stretch the lead shank a few inches closer to him. "I'll get the brushes."

Robert sets the tea jug on top of a fencepost, hangs the lead shank over his shoulder, and trots off across the pasture.

Two mating dragonflies hover like helicopters in front of me. The movements that keep them suspended there are so tiny and fast that they seem to be floating, motionless. If either my mother or Robert were here beside me watching, I'd be embarrassed.

But I'm alone, so there is no reason to turn away. Dust floats in front of the door. The air around the dragonflies sparkles with it. I read that eighty percent of the dust you see is human skin. If that's true, I wonder whether I've breathed in any of Robert yet.

Now I turn to watch him. He stops by the fence and picks up one crab apple in each hand. Happy stops grazing and lifts her head a few inches above the grass.

I walk backwards a few steps before I pry my eyes away and turn my attention to the barn where the brushes are. I swing the door wide, step over the cinderblock foundation and into the dark barn. I go all the way in. The only light comes through cracks between the boards and the open top half of a stall door. There's a ladder nailed to the wall, leading to the hayloft. A ray of sun shines down on me, on spiderwebs, scraps of hay, crumbs of sweet feed. This triangle of white beams like a spotlight. It reminds me of the one Jesus will ride down from Heaven during the rapture.

I take the lid off the metal garbage can and get Happy a fistful of sweet feed, in case the apples don't work. The molasses-covered oats smell like something for breakfast. I grab the bucket of brushes with my free hand. Through the open barn door I see that Robert already has Happy. She's drinking from her bathtub trough. He holds the garden hose and water pours out.

On my walk over to them, I check out what's in the bucket—a curry comb and a can of fly spray, a bag of rubber bands like the ones worn by people with braces, and faded red ribbon.

I want to show Robert I'm not afraid to stand behind a horse. "I'll start with the tail," I tell him, holding up the mane comb. "She never comes to me that easy," I add.

"It was the apples."

Robert chooses the hoof pick. He's a gentleman, volunteers to do the dirty work. I'm impressed.

He starts with her back leg. She makes it easy for him, bends her hoof at the ankle so he can get to the mud and manure. He's been around horses before.

Happy gets a whiff of the strong, sweet smell of the molasses and oats in my pocket. She flares her nostrils and turns her head toward her tail. She whinnies, throws her nose in the air. She demands sweet feed.

I move to Happy's mane and Robert walks to get the iced tea. He hooks the jug on a bent finger and carries it back across the pasture, squinting into the bright sun, watching me comb Happy's mane.

Standing beside me, Robert unscrews the cap and takes a long drink. He takes the jug down from his mouth and tea drips onto his chest. He doesn't wipe it off. He passes the jug. The sun makes the tea glow like a huge chunk of amber my parents and I saw at the Smithsonian.

I shake the jug side to side, mix the melted ice with the tea. I wipe off the mouth of it with the tail of my T-shirt and take my own long drink. Like all good iced tea, it's still cold and supersweet, a thirst-quenching dessert. I drink slower than Robert, trying not to gulp or drip this time. I pass the jug back. He takes an even longer drink. When it's my turn again, I suck so hard the sides of the milk jug cave in. I stare over his shoulder, at a pair of cardinals on the barbed-wire fence. The female is rust-colored, almost orange—so much prettier than the male's perfect scarlet.

Robert takes the bag of rubber bands from the bucket, gets one band out, and holds it in his teeth. Then he separates a section of Happy's mane from the rest and divides it into three equal strands.

I know how to braid. Whenever John and Judy Young come over, their daughter Trina lets me braid her hair for hours. I tried to braid Happy's hair once but gave up. It was too stiff.

Robert clamps down on the braid between his finger and thumb to keep it tight while he crosses the free strand over. All ten of his fingers move together like mechanical spiders' legs. How can he concentrate with our shoulders touching?

After he has finished a few braids, he offers me a little section of Happy's mane and says, "Here, you try." He doesn't let go of the hair he's holding until I have taken it from him. Then he moves behind me and reaches around, takes my hands in his.

"Like this," he says through the rubber band in his teeth. His fingers guide mine. We work together on the braid. It's hard to tell whose fingers are whose. We get to the end of the strand and Robert takes the rubber band from between his teeth, twists it around the braid. I pull a new section of Happy's mane between my fingers and start my next braid. Robert pulls another rubber band from the bag.

My grandmother's hair was way past her waist. I used to watch my grandfather comb and braid it every night before they got into bed. Robert's fingers move like his.

Robert steps back and stands with his arms crossed over his chest, watches to be sure I've got it. I am careful to braid just the way he did. Then he steps beside me. We work side by side. We work fast. I watch Robert watch me. I lose hold of the braid I'm working on and he smiles. I don't care that I have to take this one out and start the whole thing over.

As we get close to the end of her neck, the braids shorten. The last ones are only a few inches long. We don't speak or stop until we have braided every inch of Happy's mane. I am sad to watch Robert twist the last miniature rubber band.

Happy curves her long neck toward Robert. Our braids rock back and forth. She nudges him with her nose, nibbles his jeans, snorts her hot breath on our legs. Happy looks like one of those show horses that jump tall fences.

CHAPTER FOUR

I'm meeting Robert at Mr. Red's barn again today. We're going to ride Happy.

Momma and Daddy have usually left by the time I come upstairs to take my shower, Daddy to his church study and Momma on her job hunt. I just wait until I hear the screen door shut the second time, behind whoever leaves last, and then I have the place to myself. This morning I wait and wait, but the screen door never slams shut. Finally I have to go up, because if I wait one minute more I'll never beat Robert to Mr. Red's barn.

My plan is to gulp down an Instant Breakfast on my way out the door, maybe eat a banana on the walk over. I want to have Happy brushed, bridled, and braided, ready to ride, by the time Robert gets to the barn.

So much for my plan—the table is set for three when I get upstairs. Daddy is finishing his last few bites of breakfast. Momma's place at the table is set but untouched. Her juice glass, which used to be a jelly jar, is still full. It sweats, leaving a wet ring on the tablecloth.

With her spatula Momma lifts an egg-fried-in-bread off

her cast-iron skillet and lowers it onto my plate. She made my favorite breakfast, the one I always ask for on my birthday. If I don't eat it, don't sop up the egg yoke with the last bite of toast, she'll add that to her growing list of ways I'm not myself lately. I fork up bite after bite of my egg-fried-in-bread, dragging each one through my grits.

I am dressed for our ride. I'm wearing the exact same red gym shorts with white trim that Linda Ronstadt wears on her album cover. Except hers are silk boxer's trunks and mine are plain cotton.

Momma looks at my legs, at how little of them are covered by my shorts. And I haven't even rolled them up at the waist yet, to make them shorter. She nudges the back of my chair. *Scoot under,* she says with her knee. *Cover yourself.*

"You two boys sure have been spending a lot of time together." When Momma says *a lot of time,* she means *too much time.* She doesn't expect me to answer her, to speak up and defend my right to be with Robert as much as I please. She's making it crystal-clear, once and for all, forever and ever amen, that she doesn't want us spending so much time together.

After our first trip to Mr. Red's barn, Momma didn't bring up Robert's sinful dancing. She didn't warn me to be careful around him. She didn't seem bothered when I asked if I could go to his house or if he could come over. She didn't even flinch when I told her we'd been listening to records in his bedroom or watching TV in the basement. I told her and Daddy about our ride on the minibike Robert got for his eighth birthday, and they laughed when I described us with our knees past our ears.

But the more time I spend with him, the more I say about our plans or what we've done that day, the less she seems to like it. Now Momma bristles whenever I mention Robert. And I can't stop talking about him. Last night, while we were washing dishes, I was repeating something funny he had said, and Momma told me to hush. I could tell she hadn't meant to say it.

"Can I fry you another egg?" Momma asks Daddy. He puts his hand on her spatula hand. They're in this together, ganging up on me. He has never told me to hush, but when I come home from Robert's and he asks me how things went, he no longer sounds like he means it. He sounds like he wishes he could catch us smoking or drinking or doing something so horrible that he could forbid us to see each other ever again.

I know they think we're gay boys doing what gay boys do together. There isn't any other explanation for their growing coldness.

They probably sat propped up in bed until the wee hours of the morning and planned the breakfast sermon. They've figured out some way to say, *Don't see him anymore.* They're going to tell me to make other friends, too. Not to put all my eggs in one basket, or some other stupid saying.

Momma puts the skillet in the sink and turns on the water. The cast iron sizzles and steams. She reaches behind her and unties her apron strings. She's wearing the one with the red rooster on it over the navy blue suit Daddy bought for her when we moved to Lynchburg and she had to find a job there. The only other time she wears it is to funerals.

"Make sure you're home in time to help me get dinner on the table," Daddy says to me. Without ever saying it, he reminds me that I was late for dinner last night and the night before. "I'm cooking bologna stroganoff and I need you to make a salad."

If Robert were any not-gay boy from Sunday school, Daddy and Momma would be thrilled I made a new friend so quick. Momma would bend over backwards getting me to spend time with him. She'd have Robert and me spending so much time together we'd get sick of each other.

Sunday's about the only day I didn't see Robert. He and his mom and dad pulled their boat to the lake. I could have gone with them that day, too. Mrs. Ingle invited me to come along. She even offered to call my mom. I told her I'd ask, but I never did. Telling little lies doesn't even seem like a sin anymore. I just didn't want my parents to know that the Ingles skip church to go to the lake. It's one of Daddy's pet peeves—born-again Christians who come to church faithfully all year and then spend their summer Sundays at Smith Mountain Lake, skiing in skimpy bathing suits behind speed-boats and leaving his church pews empty.

Momma hangs Granny's rooster apron over the back of her chair and sits down. "Will you pass me the sausage?" she says. There is a mountain of untouched cheese grits on Momma's plate. The pool of butter on top has already started to turn hard.

Momma tucks her napkin into the neck of her blouse. She drizzles Karo syrup over her sausage patties, over her egg-fried-in-bread. With one hand, she cuts bites with her fork.

She leans over her plate to eat, to catch any syrup that drips.

She and Daddy look at each other. *Tell him,* her eyes say. *No, you tell him,* his eyes say back. Back and forth with the eyes. Neither of my parents says an actual word.

Momma flips through her steno pad with her free hand, rips out today's chore list, and hands it to me. Across the top of the page she's written VINCENT'S CHORE LIST in all capital letters and underlined it. Today's list is more than twice as long as yesterday's. Dust the baseboards. Trim grass from the sidewalk edges. Nothing that really needs to be done. I'll never get it finished and still meet Robert at the barn. I'll be lucky to get it done before Jesus comes back.

I watch Daddy out of the corner of my eye as he rinses his plate. Will he leave without delivering the sermon? Momma watches me. She stabs her last bite of sausage and swirls it around in her syrup and in the yolk, blends the yellow and the dark brown.

Daddy walks back to the table, leans over my shoulder, and points to my chore list. I smell his Brut aftershave. "Get this stuff done before you and the Ingle boy go ride Mr. Evans' horse," he says. As if he doesn't remember Happy's name or Robert's. When he's halfway out the door he says over his shoulder, "Y'all be good." Can't he just say what he really means?

Momma carries her plate to the screen door and watches Daddy walk across the parking lot. Then something triggers her, probably Daddy closing the church door behind him, and she turns quickly back toward me.

"Good luck on your job hunt," I blurt, hoping to remind her what a caring son she raised. Even if he is a homosexual.

Her face softens until I see a hint of smile. "I need it." Momma starts tucking her blouse into her skirt. "Luck or a miracle," she adds. "I'll take whichever one I can get."

Momma leans over me to pick up her purse from the center of the table. She presses against my shoulder while she zips it shut. The navy polyester of her blazer is cool on my bare skin. She threads her hand through the wooden handles of her purse and it dangles on her arm.

She buttons her suit coat, folds her hands, and leans back to inspect me. She pulls my wings back from my forehead and kisses me once on each eyelid. Now I'll have to check the mirror again to make sure she didn't leave any lipstick. My eyelids tingle where her lips were. They cool as air evaporates the moisture she left behind.

"Change your pants," she says. "The saddle will rub your legs raw." She says it like I don't know this, like this is what she'd been planning to say all along. What she doesn't know is that today there will be no saddle. Today, Robert and I are riding bareback.

I don't change my shorts. While I check my eyelids in the mirror for traces of red lipstick, I roll up the elastic waistband and turn my Linda Ronstadt shorts into hot pants.

I don't do the first thing on Momma's list. As soon as she's on the highway, I am out the front door. I'll work on her list of chores when I get back.

I've beaten Robert to the barn.

Happy is caked in red mud. I tie her to the hitching post and brush her down. I want to be done grooming before Robert gets here. Happy stands by the bathtub, shining, one back leg raised on its hoof. She dozes in the sun. I don't have time to weave her whole mane into braids, but I do put in a few.

Whatever she is dreaming makes her eyelids flutter. Elizabeth Taylor would kill for those lashes. I check every horseshoe nail in all four of Happy's hooves. If she throws a shoe on our ride, we'll have to walk back to the barn. I won't get to have Robert there behind me, or feel his hands on my waist the way he felt mine on his when we rode the minibike. I put down her last hoof. Done. I'm ready for our ride.

Robert calls my name from the far side of the pasture. He has one foot perched on the bottom rail of the fence, ready to lift his weight over. It's like he practiced this pose. He has on a western flannel shirt with the sleeves cut off. I'm not the only one who planned my outfit.

I want to call to him, "Howdy, handsome." But he might think I'm poking fun at his cowboy clothes.

He jogs across the pasture. His pearl buttons twinkle in the sun. The edges where the sleeves used to be attached have unraveled, and the white fringe bounces as he runs.

Momma's right to worry. There is something going on. It's not what she thinks, but it's something. We haven't held hands or kissed yet, but I have the kind of crush on Robert Ingle that I've faked since Cindy Mae became my first girl-friend in third grade. Having girlfriends didn't shield me from all torment, but it helped.

He's finally on my side of the pasture. Faded Levi's and cowboy boots. He was smart not to wear that cowboy hat I saw in his closet. It would have been too much.

I grab a handful of Happy's mane and jump. I drape over her, my belly cut in half by her spine. I hang there a second, then swing my leg over and pull myself all the way up onto her back. Happy takes a step sideways. "Whoa, girl."

Robert walks to the fencepost where I left the bucket of brushes hanging. He dumps brushes and fly spray and rubber bands and ribbon onto the ground and turns the bucket upside down next to Happy. He's so tall he could probably get on her without any help, but with the bucket, he just has to rest his hand on my shoulder for balance and climb on.

Happy's a draft horse. Mr. Red says half Shire, half Percheron. Our weight doesn't faze her. I look down and watch the ground pass underneath us. The white hair around Happy's ankles is long and fluffy. It floats and falls like my feathered bangs. She has a few years on her, but she's not swaybacked. There's just a natural curve to her spine that all horses have.

With no saddle to separate us, Robert settles in behind me, tight against me. I hold both reins in one hand and rest that hand on my knee. I lay my other hand palm down on the inside of my thigh, for balance. The way they ride in old Westerns.

Gravity pulls Robert and me together in the middle of Happy's back, him behind me, his stomach and chest against my spine. I feel every breath he takes. Robert sits just right. He doesn't hold on tight or squeeze and pull when the ride gets rough. He learned that riding minibikes.

Happy follows the logging road; I don't even have to steer. I drop the reins. We ride and ride and don't talk. It's a different kind of not talking than Momma and Daddy and I were doing before we left the house. Now I'm not speaking because I don't want to say or do anything that might mess up how perfect this moment is.

The farther we ride, the steeper the road slopes down toward the creek. The incline pushes Robert even tighter against me. Now we're only about as far from the creek as it is from home plate to first base. As the road gets steeper, Happy carries her head lower and lower until her neck is parallel to the ground. She pauses before each step. She paws the ground with a hoof, tests it before she puts all her weight down. Her sweat is making horsehair stick to the inside of my legs. Usually it would gross me out to have Happy's hair sticking to me like this, but right now nothing matters.

Happy slow-steps the last few yards. At the bank, she stops dead in her tracks. I slide and grab hold of her mane, try to keep myself from falling. Robert tightens his grip on my waist, then catches me by the upper arm and pulls me all the way back onto Happy.

Robert points to something on our right. "When I was little, my grandmother taught us how to catch those." It isn't until Robert speaks that I realize how long we've been silent.

"Catch what?"

"Those," he says. He lays the whole weight of his arm on my shoulder and points again, to honeysuckle vines covered with Japanese beetles. More beetles swarm in front of the honeysuckle. Some ride others piggyback while they mate.

Robert rests his head in the curve of my shoulder. His chin pushes against my collarbone. It hurts, but I don't say a word.

There's very little sun, but the beetles shine anyway—a layer of gold over dark green and deep purple.

We watch for a while before he says, "She taught us to tie one end of a long thread around a back leg." I can feel his Adam's apple vibrate, feel him take a deep breath to go on. "You tie the other end of the string to your finger, and when you let them go, they fly round and round in perfect circles, buzzing like hell. It sounds like a jet plane." It's the first time I've heard him use a curse word.

"Does it work if you tie the string to a front leg?" I ask. Now that we're talking, I want to keep it going.

"Only a back leg." He goes on without me needing to ask him another question. "Either back leg. The trick is to make a slipknot first, before you even catch the beetle. That way you can just slip it over the leg and pull tight."

"How do you get the string off when you're done?"

"You don't." Robert leans back and talks into my ear. He almost whispers, like he's trying to keep a secret from the Japanese beetles. "They pull so hard flying those perfect circles, eventually you're left with only a string and a back beetle leg."

I should be turned off by his cruelty, but I'm not.

I had planned for us to get off here, to let Happy graze this creek bottom while we hung our clothes from tree branches and went for a swim. The creek is not really deep enough to swim in, but I had imagined Robert and me up to our knees at least, splashing around in saggy wet underwear, kicking cold creek water on each other. Now that we're here, together on Happy, I don't want to get off, to be that far apart.

"Do the legs always come off?" I say.

"No," he says. "Sometimes you get bored first and let the beetle go, string and all."

I wonder how long it takes before the string gets tangled up in a honeysuckle vine. I don't say anything, but then I worry that Robert will think I'm judging him. I hurry to tell him, "It's not as bad as pulling the glowers off lightning bugs and sticking them all over your body."

"We used to make jewelry out of them," he answers. "Earrings, bracelets. It's kind of sick when you think about it."

I'm jealous of whoever the other half of his *we* is. "I loved making them into diamond rings. I'd put one on every finger."

I pick up Happy's reins and move them closer to her ears so she can drink as much water as she needs. When she's done, she turns her head to look at me, asks, *What next?* I nudge her with my heels but don't bother taking the reins. She back-steps up the bank and turns for the clearing.

It is this spot where I imagined Robert and me stretched out on our backs in the grass, hands under our heads, watching clouds—following fluffy dinosaurs and pirate ships sailing across the blue sky.

Happy stops and grazes in the tall grass. I should keep her from eating. Horses aren't supposed to eat when they've got a bit in their mouth. I hope she doesn't chip a tooth. We should get off and give Happy a rest.

I swing one leg over and sit sidesaddle. I turn my upper body and face Robert. Happy swats at a horsefly and her tail slaps our legs. I should have worn jeans.

Robert rubs the part of my leg Happy's tail whipped. "Did

that hurt?" He kisses two fingertips and presses them against my leg. "There," he says. "This'll make you all better." And he's right. It does. I put my hand on his shoulder to make sure he knows I'm grateful for his healing touch.

Out of nowhere, everything changes. The air cools and thickens. The earth spins slower. I know the birds don't actually quit singing, but I don't hear them anymore. The smell of honeysuckle intensifies by a factor of ten. It's like God changed the scenery, set the stage for something.

"When did you first know?" he says.

I can tell exactly what he's asking, but it's not a question I want to be answering. I don't want to answer anything. I liked it better when neither one of us was saying anything.

A horsefly bites my ankle and stays to suck blood. I take my hand off Robert's shoulder and swat hard at the fly. I miss and slap myself instead. The sting stays. I say, "Know what?" There is blood on my ankle where the horsefly bit me, and a pink patch of skin where I slapped myself trying to kill it.

Japanese beetles are everywhere. I make myself think about how cruel Robert is for tying strings to their legs.

Robert leans in and meets me eye to eye. I try to avoid his stare by looking off to the right, but when I turn back he's still staring.

"I'm gay, Vincent," he says. "And I think you're gay too."

I've never looked anyone so square in the eye. Not even myself in the mirror. Tears well up in his eyes and in mine.

I don't know where the power comes from, but it rushes like a mighty wind, and I tell Robert Ingle what I've never told another living soul, not even God.

"When I was little, my favorite outfit was this pink-and-white-striped short set. It came in a bag of hand-me-downs some church member left on our back doorstep. It was polyester knit, bubblegum pink. I loved it so much. Momma would wash it every night while I took my bath so I could wear it the next day. I refused to get into the tub until I'd seen her put it in the washing machine. If it wasn't all the way dry in the morning, I'd put it on wet.

"One day Momma and I were in the grocery store and I was wearing that pink-striped short set. The lady in line in front of us got bored waiting, so she marked her place in her magazine with her finger, turned around, and asked Momma, 'What's your pretty little girl's name?' It wasn't the first time somebody had said that.

"Momma wasn't rattled. She said, 'Vincent,' just like she always did when people confused me for a girl. Other times when that happened, the person who thought I was a girl would get embarrassed and try to make up for it by going on and on about how cute I was, how much I look like my mother, but not the woman in the grocery store that day. That woman didn't get embarrassed, she got quiet. She got mad.

"She put her magazine back in the rack and said, 'Miss. You go on dressing him like a little girl and he'll do like my boy and turn queer on you before he's half grown.'

"I'd never heard that word before, *queer*, but the second it came out of her mouth I knew she was right. I *was* one. And being one was bad. I heard all that in her voice."

"What'd your momma say to that woman?" Robert asks.

I like it that he's not freaked out. He doesn't go silent, like I just told the saddest story he's ever heard.

"She didn't say anything. The woman behind the cash register rang up her last item and asked for the money. The lady started searching her purse."

Robert's ready with another question. "What happened to the pink short set?"

"On the ride home I ripped it off and threw it over the back of the seat onto the floor. I never saw it again. I walked into the house in my underwear. I guess Momma handed it down to some other kid. Since that day in the grocery store, nothing pink."

When I'm done with my story he doesn't rush in with one of his own, doesn't try to trump mine with an even better one. We sit in silence, except for the ripple of the creek and the crunching sound of Happy ripping grass out by the root.

I want to cup my hand around the back of his head, the way Daddy does when he prays with someone at the altar, and pull Robert even closer to me. I want to kiss him, just like we are in a soap opera. I bet myself a million dollars he wouldn't pull away if I did.

Instead, I say, "What about you? When did you first know?"

CHAPTER FIVE

I point to the sign over the waitress's head. Little white letters spell out breakfast foods on a black felt background: BACON. SAUSAGE. EGG AND CHEESE SANDWICH. GRITS. To the right of each is a price. Everything's cheaper than I expected. I guess they don't overcharge people who are here to visit their sick and dying loved ones. Or maybe they have a special discount for sons of preachers who come with their fathers to make hospital visits—a discount for having to cancel the ride I was going to take with Robert.

"I'll have The Continental," I say. I can afford that.

The waitress takes a pad out of her apron pocket and pulls a pencil from her loose bun. "What kind of doughnut, hon?" Her dyed-black hair has grown snow-white roots. She must not make enough working in the hospital coffee shop to afford a dye job very often. April Johnson told me waitresses don't want people to know who they really are, so they put a fake name on their name tags. If what April Johnson says is true, this waitress is not Letty.

I feel a little guilty eating in the hospital snack bar. Everyone here is sad about someone they know who's sick.

I'm not sad. Aside from not being with Robert right now, I'm happier than I ever remember being.

If I'd gotten home from our bareback ride yesterday in time to finish the chores on Momma's list, they wouldn't have made me come with Daddy on these hospital visits, and Robert and I would be together, somewhere. In his room listening to eight-tracks. Riding Happy. Happy.

Instead, Momma left me a note: *Meet your father at his car at ten. Mom.* She stapled it to today's chore list.

On the stool beside me at the lunch counter sits a woman so round that her flabby arms rub against mine. She tells the man next to her, "He fell twenty feet onto a pile of railroad ties."

"He's lucky to be alive at all," the man answers.

"Didn't break a bone."

If anyone asks me why I'm here, who I'm visiting, I plan to say my friend was in a car wreck. I put on the same almost-in-tears face everyone around me is wearing. I miss him so much it's not hard to be convincing.

The Continental comes with coffee. They say coffee puts hair on your chest. Momma and Daddy drink pots and pots of coffee every day, but they won't let me have any. A coffee cup is turned upside down in a saucer in front of me. I turn it over. Not-Letty pours and asks, "Room for milk?"

"No," I say. "No milk." Momma takes cream and sugar. I'll drink mine black, like Daddy and other men. I blow across the coffee.

My breath makes ripples in the surface. I expect the coffee to burn my tongue, but it's barely warm. It's bitter. My tongue doesn't want it. I shake two packets of sugar back and forth fast until all the sugar is pressed tightly together in the bottom of the packet. Packed together like Robert and I were yesterday, riding bareback on Happy. Like we would be right now if they hadn't made me come here. I shake the packets faster, as if it's their fault I'm not with Robert. I tear them open and flick them with my middle finger until every last crystal is dumped into my mug.

If Momma and Daddy make me come again, I'll get Robert to borrow his mother's car and meet me here. They can't control him. I'll introduce him to Not-Letty. We'll have coffee and doughnuts and pretend somebody has cancer.

I order lemon creme because it's Robert's favorite, but the filling has a tin-can taste that the powdered sugar can't cover up. I eat every last bite anyway. I scrape my doughnut plate with the edge of my fork, getting all the lemon filling, and lick the fork clean.

"How about a hot top?" Not-Letty asks. At first I don't know what she means. I look at my cup. She's already refilled it to the brim, no room for milk. I hope she didn't see me licking the fork. "Fresh pot," she says.

I say to Not-Letty, "Just the check," the way Daddy does in restaurants. Using his words, sounding like him, reminds me that I'm still mad at Momma and him for making me come, for keeping me away from Robert.

Not-Letty takes her order pad out of her apron pocket, licks her thumb, and starts to add up the bill.

Like Kmart, this hospital has automatic doors. I guess they have to, with all the wheelchairs. Once I'm outside, I stop to figure out which direction to walk. I look at my watch. Eleven o'clock. I walk toward the shops I saw when we drove in. I don't have to meet Daddy until noon.

The outside air is thicker than the hospital air, harder to walk through, even though sickness doesn't hang as heavy. In one of the rooms behind me, my father prays with someone. My mother is somewhere, begging for a job. I don't know what Robert is doing.

I have a dollar in my pocket. I doubt I'll be able to find anything decent for Robert that only costs a dollar. Maybe a Hallmark card, some candy. If I'd known I could go shopping, I'd have brought more money. I'll window-shop instead, like Momma. Anything is better than staying where Daddy tells me to, reading *Progressive Farmer* magazines in the hospital lobby. Besides, I never get to shop alone.

It's August, but if I stay on the shady side of the street, the walk there and back won't completely kill my hairdo. Anyway, even bad hair would be better than watching crying strangers kiss goodbye, better than sitting in the lobby listening to some sick person's sister tell you how much you remind her of her son.

A man is dressing a mannequin in the window of Thompson's Haberdashery. He pulls dress fabric tight behind a mannequin's back, gives her a wasp waist, like Scarlett O'Hara in *Gone With the Wind*. He holds straight pins in his teeth the same way Momma does when she's sewing.

The next window display looks like a bookstore, but NEWS- STAND is painted on the door, in gold cursive letters outlined in black to make them look three-dimensional. I know a dollar isn't enough to buy a book, not even a Harlequin romance. I wouldn't want to give Robert a book anyway. What kind of gift is that?

Bells jingle as I open the door. It's almost as cold in the newsstand as it was in the hospital. The bells are still jingling even after I turn around and double-check that the door is shut tight so no air conditioning can leak out.

A cat meows. She paces back and forth between my ankles, rubs up against me. Straight in front of me, at the far end of the store, a Pepsi machine glows in the dark room behind a beaded curtain.

"She bothering you?" a voice asks from behind a rack of greeting cards. Even though I knew someone had to be in the store somewhere, the voice still startles me.

"No. I have a cat."

"Want another one?"

Whoever he is is being extra nice, but his little joke makes me uncomfortable. I almost turn and go. But I step deeper into the store. I see brown leather Docksiders sticking out from behind a round rack of greeting cards, the kind that spins. The man who goes with the brown shoes is straightening cards. One by one he slides cards inside their envelopes, making sure each one fits right. That's me and Robert—a perfect fit. The man squats down to work on the bottom row. When he does, his khakis tighten around his privates. I turn my head to make sure he doesn't think I'm staring.

"I'm Matt," he says. "In case you need me." Matt is too young and athletic to have so much gray hair. He's not balding one bit.

"Just browsing." Now I sound like my mother. I can't turn around and leave. I've said it, so I browse.

Matt has never built anything in those construction worker boots he wears. There isn't a scratch or a speck of red mud. If he did actually work in them, he didn't do it in that madras shirt with a sweater tied around his neck. Matt is covered in gayness, from the soles of his spotless construction-worker boots, straight up his legs in their creased jeans, all the way to the top of his hairsprayed head.

The back wall is floor-to-ceiling magazines. Row after row of them. I doubt if any cost less than a dollar. Sometimes while Momma fills up her cart with groceries, I read magazines. The Kroger doesn't have half as many as this newsstand.

I start at the far left and work my way right. I scan the covers—there are bridal magazines, magazines for parents, ones about crafts, travel, photography. A few of them I recognize from the grocery store.

"Finding anything?" Matt calls out from somewhere behind me.

One of the photography magazines has an almost naked woman on the cover. The model uses her arms and hands to cover herself. I flip through this one. There are more nudes. All are women. I feel the same way I did when I used to look at ladies' underwear in the Sears catalogue. Nothing.

The section with all the teen magazines is the biggest. *Teen Beat. Tiger Beat.* The fitness section is at the far right, on the bottom shelf. I squat down to look closer. Weight-lifting magazines, mostly. The muscle man on the cover is so blown up and shiny he looks like an alien.

Then I notice the half-size magazines peeking out from the very back of the bottom shelf. They're a little bigger than Harlequin romances and about half as thick, with paper covers. The only part of them that shows is the black lettering that stretches across the top—titles like *First Hand* and *My First Time*, *True Tail*. I lift one out of the rack so I can see all of it, then another, then another. There are pencil drawings and photographs of shirtless men. Pubic hair peeks out of every unzipped pair of jeans. Enormous penises snake down skinny legs, stop just above the knee.

They don't carry these at the grocery store.

The curtain beads rattle. I hear Matt drop change in the Pepsi machine, one coin at a time.

I keep one *First Hand* and put the others back in the rack. I can't believe what I'm holding. Me, the boy who wouldn't let himself watch *The Wild Wild West* because James and Artemis wore their jeans so tight.

The paper of the *First Hand* isn't smooth and shiny like the pages of the photography magazines. I open it hoping for naked pictures like the ones in Uncle Herb's copies of *Hustler*, only of men. But this magazine is filled mostly with stories. A couple of drawings go with each one, most of them by somebody named Tom of Finland. Since none of the men are completely naked, I'm not technically looking at pornography, which would definitely be a sin. There are advertisements for massage wands and little yellow pills called Spanish Fly and penis enlargers.

Half of me wishes Robert were here with me, that we were discovering these magazines together. Pirates digging up buried treasure. The other half of me feels like I'm being unfaithful. More to Robert than to God. It doesn't feel so much like sin. I wonder if Robert's ever looked at magazines like these, if he'd be mad that I'm looking at them. Maybe he has a whole collection in a suitcase under his bed, like my old collection of *Richie Rich* comic books.

I look over my shoulder. There's no sign of Matt. The beads haven't rattled again. Lightning hasn't struck. I start to read a story, "Kentucky Blue Balls." I pick that particular one because Daddy went to seminary in Kentucky. It's where he learned to preach.

I'm not halfway through the first paragraph when the bells above the door jingle. In the time it takes the cat to meow— that quick—I decide to steal the book. I'm not torn about what to do; I just do it. It's not until *First Hand* is stuffed down my pants and my shirt is pulled over it that I have a single thought of hell, where I'll definitely go if I keep this up. Momma and Daddy made me come to the hospital to keep me away from my perfectly innocent times with Robert, to protect me from my sinful self. And here I am, shoplifting a magazine with pictures of almost naked men.

The beaded curtain rattles. "Let me know if I can help you find anything," Matt says to whoever just entered. I stand up and suck my stomach in. I baby-step my way around, careful not to dislodge the magazine. I look out over bookshelves and greeting-card racks. The new customer is the round woman from the snack bar. Her purse is draped over her forearm, just like Momma's. She waves at me with that hand. She remembers me. I pretend I don't remember her.

The magazine slides down a few inches. Its sharp edges cut into me. I'm afraid to take my next step.

I watch Matt and the round woman say a few words. He leads her toward the far wall. Their backs are to me. This is my chance. I hold my arm across my stomach like I have a bellyache, hold the magazine tight against me. Nervous sweat sticks the magazine to my skin. I keep my eyes glued to Matt and the woman while I do the *I've-got-to-go-to-the-bathroom-really-bad* baby step across the newsstand. The bells over the door jingle, the cat meows, and I'm out of there.

The entire ride home, the magazine cuts into me. I hope it hasn't broken the skin and drawn blood.

When we get back home, Daddy and I part ways. He heads across the church parking lot to his study and I head for my room. Momma's car isn't under the carport. She must still be job hunting.

As soon as I am through the kitchen door, before I pull the *First Hand* out of my pants, I look over my shoulder to make sure Daddy hasn't changed his mind and come home. There's a bathroom at the church, but he still comes home when he has to go.

I'm alone, so I pull out the magazine and inspect it. It doesn't look brand-new anymore. This makes me a little sad. The cover is wrinkled. At least there are no permanent creases, nothing the iron won't smooth out. The cover is wet with my sweat. I dry it on my T-shirt. The edges of the inside pages are wet, darkened.

I wonder if the owner of the newsstand will make Matt

pay for the stolen magazine out of his next paycheck. Or maybe Matt is the owner. I guess there aren't any laws against gays owning their own businesses. A lot of florists and hairdressers do.

The next time I have to go with Daddy on his hospital visits, I'll repay the money, leave it on the shelf where the magazine was. Maybe I'll even get up the nerve to buy another one. I'm pretty sure it's illegal to purchase magazines with pictures of almost naked people until you're eighteen, but Matt might not ask to see proof of my age.

I feel guiltier about stealing than I do about what I've stolen.

I go down to my room. Now to get comfortable. I unbutton my Levi's, unzip them, but stay dressed the rest of the way. I even keep my fake Chuck Taylors on.

I crawl onto my bottom bunk, slide under the covers. Immediately I can tell I will be too hot, so I throw off my comforter, leaving only the sheet. I point my knees to the underside of the top bunk and pull my heels back until they touch my butt cheeks. The sheet makes a tent. I put my thumbs under the elastic waistband of my underwear. I spread my feet out wide, almost to the edges of the mattress, press into them, and raise myself up off the bed. I scoot my underwear and jeans over my hips, slide them down my thighs. I stop just below my knees. The bottom sheet is soft on my butt. The air under the sheet is cool against my skin.

I turn to the table of contents. While I read the titles, I discover how easy it is to hold this little magazine with one hand. How convenient. Genius even. I turn on the reading light that is clipped to one of the top bunk slats. I hold my first *First Hand* open with both hands, the same way I read novels for English class. I adjust the angle of the lamp so it makes a perfect spotlight on a Tom of Finland drawing. I rest my forearms on my slanted thighs. When Momma and Daddy gave me that reading lamp for my birthday last year, I'm sure they imagined me staying up to read my new Living Bible.

Now I'm here with "Cowboy in a Quandary," a story about a ranch hand who gets fired for fooling around with the ranch owner's son. He fools around with a bunch of other cowboys, too. Reading this is like reading any other story. It draws me into its world. Captures me and holds me there, deep in it. The only difference is that this is a world I've never seen in print, a world of mouths and bodies and the perfect apartment with the perfect piece of furniture for each different homosexual act the men commit. *Commit.* The same word people use for suicide. Or murder. I'm not sure I want to do all the things these men are doing, and they definitely talk too much while they're doing it, but I don't see the crime. Everybody seems to be having a good time. No one gets hurt.

But I wish these characters were more real, more romantic. Every one of them is perfect, right down to his foot-long penis. These men aren't in love; they barely know each other. They do their business and part ways without even a goodbye. Not a one of them is afraid to burn in hell for eternity.

I have read "Cowboy in a Quandary" twice now and I still don't know what the cowboy was in a quandary over. I am reading "Lawyer Lust" for the second time when I hear

Momma's VW Beetle come up the driveway and park under the carport.

After dinner I offer to do the dishes, even though it isn't my night. Momma answers, "You've done enough for one day." Boy, have I.

I stretch my arms over my head, fake-yawn, and say, "I think I'm going to hit the hay," exactly what Daddy says almost every night. Only he doesn't say it at six-thirty. It doesn't even get dark until almost nine.

Momma and Daddy raise their eyebrows together, like they've planned it. Like water ballerinas they tilt the tops of their heads in my direction—two dogs hearing the same noise. They don't buy it.

I bring my arms down to my stomach and add, "That cabbage isn't sitting too well." *Sitting well*—more of Daddy's exact words.

"Wouldn't surprise me, the way you wolfed it down," Daddy says.

"Chewing is the first stage of digestion," Momma adds. "Your stomach can't do all the work."

I'm worse than a kid trying to play hooky. I might as well put shoe polish under my tongue to raise my temperature. I once believed that worked, too.

I know Momma and Daddy will come downstairs at seven to watch *Jeopardy* like they do every night, but as soon as I get to my room I take my *First Hand* out from its hiding place between the mattress and the box springs. I crawl under the covers and bend my legs into their tent position. This time, I pull my jeans all the way off and throw them on the floor.

Momma and Daddy come downstairs for their date with *Jeopardy*. I can tell they're whispering about something, but I can't make out what it is. The TV goes on. The *Jeopardy* theme song plays. One of them knocks on my door.

"Vincent." It's Momma. "Do you want to watch TV with us?" I shove the magazine back under my mattress.

"Not tonight," I say. "I want to watch *Charlie's Angels* at nine."

"We won't count it against your two hours."

The last thing I want is to be in the same room with them, but she's not taking no for an answer. "Okay. I'll be right out."

I get up and pull my pants on, check myself in the full-length mirror that hangs by my door. My cheeks are pink, but there's no other sign of what I've been doing. She'll still be able to tell something's up.

I open the door and there's Momma, holding a plate of sugar cookies and a glass of milk.

CHAPTER SIX

Robert and I ride Happy to the top of White Oak Mountain. No saddle. The way up is so steep I have to grip hard with my knees and grab a handful of Happy's mane just to stay on.

"You go ahead," Robert says and nods to the fire tower visible above the trees. "I'll tie her and be right up."

I hate to leave him behind, but I do what he says.

The tower is a metal triangle that's been cut off at the top. The mutant son of the Washington Monument and the Eiffel Tower. The paint is so faded I can't tell if it was originally blue or green, but the color of everything else around me— the dirt road, the trees, the buzzing bees—seems turned way up. Long, flat beams crisscross each other. Rusted bolts hold them in place.

I'm surprised the stairs that lead up to the tower aren't blocked off. When Robert told me that we were coming here to celebrate my birthday, I pictured us having to climb over a tall rusty fence to get in, but it's like there is an open invitation for us to go on up. There's even a handrail. The metal is cold.

Halfway up, the stairs stop, replaced by ladders, which

are harder to climb. The railing is gone. I'm okay until I get above the tree line. It's windy up here. The tower sways. A plywood platform sits at the very top. There is no railing. I wonder if anyone's ever been blown off.

The treetops below are a sloping green carpet. I can see the church steeple and the roof of the parsonage. It looks like Matchbox cars are driving up White Oak Mountain. We're here on top of the world, like Karen Carpenter sings.

Over my shoulder, I see that Robert has started his climb. From up here he looks small. But so romantic. I know he can't hear me, so I sing Karen's song out loud. Robert's love has put me on the top of the world.

I haven't told him about the magazine yet. I don't know why I'm afraid to; we talk about other things and so far nothing I've said has turned him off. I don't know if it's a sin to keep secrets, but it sure feels like one. Still, I'm not going to confess today and ruin this picnic he planned just for me.

I kneel on the platform and rein in my fear of being in bird land without a railing. I lift one foot first to get my balance before I stand all the way up. The platform sinks a little under my weight.

Robert pokes his head and neck through the square opening. "Any trouble?" he says.

"Nope."

He takes his newspaper delivery bag off his shoulder and sets it on the platform. Things clink together. He does not kneel first. He climbs right to his feet. Sweat outlines his ribcage.

I study the shape and size of each lump in his *Star Tribune* bag in an attempt to figure out what his idea of a birthday picnic is. Since we met today at Mr. Red's barn, I've smelled what can only be fried chicken. I wonder if he was the cook.

Robert takes a yellow towel from his bag and spreads it out. I watch him unpack our picnic. There are three pastel Tupperware containers. Small, medium, and large. Pink, sky blue, and mint green.

The large pink one is full of the fried chicken I suspected. I can see it through the plastic lid. The last thing he takes out is a quart-size Ball jar of iced tea. He unscrews the lid. "I didn't bring any glasses," he says, holding the jar out to me. "I thought we could share."

I take it from him and suck down a long drink.

"Happy birthday to you," he sings. *Happy birthday to me.*

Robert stops unpacking even though there are still two lumps in the bag. I wonder if one is a present.

We eat the drumsticks first, then the thighs. I don't really like dark meat, so I cover the taste of each bite with biscuit or a forkful of potato salad. Between bites, I gulp tea, try to wash the stringy meat down. I pass the jar to Robert. The chicken grease on our hands makes the glass hard to hold.

The chicken is cold on my fingers, on my tongue. It was probably fried yesterday and kept in the fridge overnight. The biscuits are still warm enough to melt butter, but he didn't bring any.

We do not talk, we eat. We chew and look out over the treetops. We swallow and smile at each other. I couldn't care less that there were no chicken breasts. When Robert has taken his last bite, he pulls up a corner of the towel and wipes his mouth on it. "Sorry I forgot the napkins. Do you want dessert first, or your present?"

I almost blurt out *Present*, but I stop myself. I don't want to sound greedy. Whatever he got me, it's the perfect gift.

The wind makes the tower sway again. The metal beams squeak. They're welded together with bolts as big as my arm that must have been here for years and years. That's how connected I am to Robert. I don't need a present or dessert. This is ten times more than I ever thought I'd have.

Robert reaches into the bag. He decides for me. My eyes follow the movement of his hand under the canvas.

I can tell immediately that what he pulls out is an eight-track tape. He has wrapped it in pink tissue paper. The exact color pink of that striped, hand-me-down short set. There is no bow, one less thing to keep me from it.

The tissue paper is fragile, and even though I'm careful lifting each piece of tape, I still tear it in a few places.

"Sorry," he says. He has just given me the best birthday of my life. There is nothing he could have done that would require an apology. This moment is perfect.

"For what?"

He points to the eight-track tape. "I couldn't help but listen to it." Now I notice the tape is not shrink-wrapped. "I know that's tacky," he says.

The wind tries to snatch the paper out of my hands. Robert takes it from me and smooths it out against his chest. The loose corners flap in the breeze.

He bought me Barry Manilow, *This One's for You*. The perfect name for a birthday gift. Except for his eyes, Barry's not that cute. His eyebrows have been plucked. His hair curves around his face. There's no way he got it to do that without a curling iron. I turn the eight-track over. "Copacabana" is not on *This One's for You*. There is a second photograph of Barry. In it he's sitting in a recording studio with his eyes closed. His legs are crossed knee over knee, like a girl.

"Happy birthday," Robert says.

"Thank you." I should say more, should lean across the empty Tupperware, cup my hand around the back of his neck, and thank him properly, with a kiss. Instead, I reach out and take the pink tissue paper back, unfold it. I use both hands to keep the wind from snatching it.

I hold the pink paper by two corners. The paper flies like a flag. I raise it high over my head. We both watch it whip in the wind, bubblegum pink against a white-blue sky. I feel light enough to be lifted off the tower.

The sun shines through the tissue paper, almost like a stained-glass window. The wind tries harder and harder to steal it from me. We both watch.

I hope Robert doesn't think I'm a litterbug, but I have to see the tissue paper fly. I let go with only my right hand first. The pink rectangle becomes a flapping flame, leaping up to God. I let go with my left. The paper lifts. It does not sink and land on a treetop. It lifts higher, higher. Up, up, and away. Over the treetops.

"Happy birthday to me," I say.

We get caught in a rainstorm on our ride back down White Oak Mountain. Since I know Momma and Daddy are at the

hospital, visiting the sick, I suggest that we stop at the parsonage first. Robert can shower while I dry his clothes. Just
as Happy sensed the storm, I smell the danger in my own
plan, but I proceed anyway.

I tie Happy under the carport, out of the rain, and then
help Robert empty his newspaper bag, spread things out to
dry—everything but my Barry Manilow eight-track, which
I won't let go of.

Before we even go inside to dry off, the sun is forcing
itself through the black clouds.

It is dark in our hallway except for a crack under Momma
and Daddy's bedroom door. A triangle of light, the same
shape as the fire tower, leaks out into the hall.

Instead of flipping on the switch, I cover it with my hand.
A full-length mirror hangs on the linen closet door, at the
end of the hall. I don't want to watch my drenched self walk
toward it. I don't want Robert to watch me either. My clothes
are glued to my skin. My hair drips. I lick a few drops from
my upper lip. It tastes like Aqua Net. I know my wings have
drooped onto my forehead. I can barely see through them.
Robert is a half step behind me. His hand is on my shoulder
like we are doing the Bunny Hop. He breathes on my neck. I
lead him to Momma and Daddy's bathroom but do not follow
him all the way in.

"Our only shower is in here," I say, pointing through the
open door. "My bathroom just has a tub." When I made my
plan, I didn't think how weird it would be to have him naked
in my parents' shower, the shower I use every morning,
drying himself with towels I use.

I pass Robert a washcloth and take one step backward into Momma and Daddy's bedroom before I pull the door almost all the way closed. I leave my hand on the knob and watch Robert through the crack. He turns on the shower and lets the water run while he pulls his Miss Pac-Man T-shirt over his head and off.

I cannot see what Robert sees in the mirror, only his back side, his dripping hair. There is a small curve of soft flesh just above his belt and peach fuzz in the small of his back, above his wet Levi's.

Robert takes a step backward and reaches his hand into the shower to test the water. I stretch my arm through the crack, into the room, and wait for him to hand me his wet T-shirt.

"Pass me your clothes and I'll put them in the dryer," I remind him. I hate to break the silence. I could keep watching him, but I don't want to get caught.

Our hands touch when Robert passes me the T-shirt. Without untying his Chuck Taylors, he toes one off, then the other. He's not wearing socks. The only thing left to come off is his jeans.

I breathe the steam from the shower. Robert unbuckles his belt and pulls it out of its loops. He rolls it up like a snake, then tucks it into a sneaker.

"Here," he says, handing me both Chucks.

"Thank you," I say. I hold both of them in one hand and loosen the strings, pull the tongues out with the other.

Robert unfastens the top button of his Levi's. I sit his sneakers on the floor behind me and stretch my hand back into the steamy bathroom, palm up. He doesn't turn around; he stays facing me. I feel his eyes on me but can only stare at the tile floor. Robert undoes another button, and before I can turn my head, I see white underwear.

The thing I turn to is Momma and Daddy's wedding portrait. I just shut my eyes and wait.

I put on dry clothes—my old gym shorts and a blue mesh shirt. I put our wet clothes in the dryer. Together. I wait in my room for Robert to finish his shower. If Momma were here, she'd be complaining about how much hot water Robert is wasting.

I light a cone of incense and both of the drip candles I made last year at church camp. I unscrew the bulb in my overhead light. I lie on my back on my bottom bunk and listen to the metal buttons on Robert's jeans clanging against the inside of the dryer. I remember Barry Manilow and go back upstairs to get my tape. The shower is still running.

I go downstairs and put Barry in the eight-track player Momma and Daddy gave me for my birthday. I am barely stretched out on my bottom bunk again when the water stops running through the pipes overhead. I wait, listen to Robert clomp down the hallway and call me from the top of the stairs.

I play dead. I want him to have to search for me, for him to find me down here in the candlelight. I hear his footsteps overhead. The screen door opens, closes. He's checking to see if I'm out with Happy. I wait for him and listen to his buttons clang, clang, clang.

"Vincent," he calls again from the top of the stairs. He flicks the switch on and off the way Momma does when she's trying to wake me up in the morning. I don't answer. "Vincent?" he says again, this time with a question mark. He starts downstairs and I still stay dead—but up on my elbows, my eyes wide open, so I can see him when he takes his first step into my bedroom.

He opens the door and stands like a Sears catalogue model in my doorway, my terry-cloth bathrobe tied tight at his waist. The sleeves are a little short. I almost gave him Daddy's bathrobe, but that would have been too weird.

He tightens the knot of his belt. Barry starts his second song.

Robert does not ask permission to join me. He stretches out beside me like we've done this a million times. Our arms and hands and hips and thighs are seamed together. There is a sad gap just above our ankles.

"Put it on 'All the Time,'" he says.

I lean up on my elbows. I'm about to get up and change the track, but his bathrobe is open almost to his waist, and this time I stop and look. I have to strain to see him in this dim light. His collarbones are showing, and a foot-wide strip of his chest. The robe comes back together just above his belly button. A thin line of hair grows up his stomach, reaches for his Adam's apple.

Robert lifts up on his own elbow. "It's the first cut on track four," he says, and lies back down. I like the way he uses the word *cut* like a record producer.

I get up and change the track. *Click. Click.* With each click, a different green dot lights up, lets me know which track I'm on. I lie back down on the bed. I feel the heat he soaked up in the shower. There is no steam down here, but the air is still hard to breathe. I get a whiff of the incense.

An hour ago we were watching pink paper float across White Oak Mountain. Not five minutes ago he was naked in my parents' shower. Now he's here next to me, in my bathrobe, on my bed.

The tape squeaks and turns inside the player. The buttons of the jeans clang inside the clothes dryer. Everything has its sound. I wait for the song to start.

Finally, an instrumental introduction. Strings. Piano and cello, I think. Usually Barry has long orchestral introductions, but this one plays only a few measures before the first lyrics.

Barry sings about thinking he was the only one, that he was crazy like no one else. Why did Robert choose this song for us? Is he trying to tell me Barry's thoughts are his own? I push my hip, the side of my thigh tight against him, let him know I also used to think I was the only one.

Not that I ever thought I was the only gay. Just the only one who was not some kind of a pervert. The only one who's not a hairdresser or a florist, not a big sissy queer like in all the movies. Not only out for sex like the men in my *First Hand* magazine.

Barry sings about how he would have given everything he owns just for someone to tell him he's not alone. That's exactly how I used to feel down at the altar. I would have given everything I own for God to deliver me from my homosexuality. But right now I want as many moments like this as I can get.

Robert takes my hand. We interlock fingers. He rubs my palm with his thumb, back and forth like a windshield wiper. With his thumb he says, *You're not alone. You have me now. I'm not alone anymore either.* I turn my head to him. He stares above us, at the bottom of the top bunk. His profile is perfect in the candlelight. He mouths the words as Barry sings the chorus, sings about wasting years waiting for a sign. Like Barry, for years I've been waiting for God to send me a sign that He's saved me, forever and ever amen. And I always thought His sign would be to change me, to take away every impure thought, wipe out every homosexual desire, make my limp wrists stiff, stop my hips from swishing when I walk. He made the lame to walk and the blind to see, raised Lazarus from the dead; surely He could save me. But now I'm thinking that maybe I had it all wrong, and maybe, just maybe, I don't need to be changed.

Robert stops rubbing my thumb and we just lie there listening to Barry.

I've never heard this song before, but I feel like if I open my mouth and start to sing along, I'll know every word. But I don't sing. This moment is sacred. I feel God move in my soul now the same way He does during an altar call. I hear His voice. Not through scripture or Daddy's sermon, but through Barry Manilow.

God knows I've given everything. He knows that for years I've come before Him with a pure heart, the way the Bible says you're supposed to, and I'm still as gay as the first time I knelt at the altar. For years, He hasn't changed me. Maybe that's my sign. Maybe He's been trying to send it to me all the time, just like Barry is saying. Maybe by refusing to change me, God has been trying to show me the truth.

As Barry sings about needing someone to tell him he's not so bad, it's as though God says those exact words to me. His message is so clear and simple I can't believe I never heard Him before. If I had stopped to listen to God earlier, instead of listening to all the other voices, I might have heard Him say that sooner.

Barry ends the song with a key change and holds the last few notes for eternity, the way he ends every song. Robert lets go of my hand and turns on his side, not just his head but his whole body. It is too dark for me to see more than shadows on his face. I cannot see his eyes, but I stare into them. I feel him stare back. We are so close our breath mixes together into a single warm cloud. I slow down my inhales and exhales so we breathe in unison.

Between songs, there is only the slow squeak of the tape turning inside the eight-track player.

The dryer stops spinning and the clothes thump down into a pile at the bottom. The metal buttons of Robert's Levi's clang for the last time. The timer buzzes.

CHAPTER SEVEN

"Momma?" I yell down the basement stairs.

"Down here." Her voice comes from the far side of the den. I can tell from her tone that something's very wrong. Robert and I ran out of gas on his Honda Trail 90. I'm late. Again. I hope that's all she's mad about.

She is sitting on the fireplace hearth. Her legs are uncrossed, her knees pinned together, shins at a forty-five-degree angle to the linoleum floor. Momma dabs her eyes with a clean corner of her dirty dust rag. She pulls the rag down below her nose, sniffs into it. She has been cleaning. I must not have done a good enough job with the things on her list.

She has been crying, but she isn't now. Her red eyes are clearing. This is not about me being late. Maybe they called from the nursing home to say Granny passed. Or something happened to Daddy.

Momma looks off to the right, over her shoulder at the dark wood paneling. Dust floats in a triangle of light that pours through the tiny basement window. She stares at that. I watch her blink back a tear, turn to face me.

The linoleum is cold through my socks. Momma starts a slow turn of her head, back toward the window. There are answers out there, help of some kind on the other side of the glass. Even more slowly, she turns her head back to me. I ask God to help me look her in the eye, but I can't.

Instead, I look down. At the coffee table, at the yellow can of Endust. It's a lie. You can never end dust. You just get rid of it and make way for a fresh layer. Beside the furniture spray is my *First Hand* magazine.

Oh my God.

My magazine is turned face down, but the back cover is all I need to see. I would know it anywhere. I look away the second I see it. If I don't look at it, maybe it will disappear.

My mind is perfectly empty. I focus on the rhythm of the blood pumping through my brain. It all begins to add up. We can no longer pretend I am what I'm not or that I'm not what I am. Daddy can never again brag that I'm going to grow up and follow him into the pulpit. Momma knows once and for all that I'll never get married and bring her grandkids home for Christmas. There's no more denying it. Satan has me. The proof is lying face down on the coffee table.

Momma clears her throat. "I called your father. He'll be right home."

I sit down on the couch facing her but not looking at her. We wait for Daddy. She stares through the floating dust out the high rectangle window. I stare at the ash bucket on the hearth.

I hear Daddy's footsteps on the driveway, then in the kitchen over our heads. Momma must hear him too, but she does nothing, says nothing. Daddy doesn't search the house looking for us. He walks straight to the top of the stairs. She told him where to find us.

Daddy rushes down. He crosses in front of me and into the center of the den. He plants both feet solidly, puts his hands on his hips. "What's so important?" he asks Momma.

Momma turns her knees to the coffee table. She uses the dust rag like a potholder and picks up the magazine. She holds it out to him. "Look what your son's been reading." After he takes my *First Hand* from her, she drops the dust rag onto the linoleum. She can't even touch the thing that's touched the magazine. "I found it under your son's mattress."

I try to think of a lie, but there's nothing to say that will get me out of this.

Daddy turns the *First Hand* over and back, thumbs through the brittle pages. In the short time since I stole it, the paper has started to yellow. Every few pages Daddy stops to read. I cannot inhale until he turns the page again. He's disgusted, I can tell. By the magazine and by his son. He knows why I have it, what I do when I read it.

"Who gave this to you?" is the first question out of Daddy's mouth. "Did that Ingle boy give you this?" I'm sure he thinks Robert and I have done the things he's reading.

They'll never let me see him again. Never let us picnic on White Oak Mountain. I'll never be allowed to go to Robert's house. Never again will I stretch out on his bedroom floor and listen to albums all afternoon. We'll never ride bareback together again. Why didn't she just clean her own bedroom?

Daddy comes around the table to face me. He tries to look me in the eye, but I stare at my feet.

"Where did you get this?" He puts one hand under my chin and lifts my eyes level with his. Does he think this will make me answer? I turn my eyes as far in their sockets as they will go. This blurs Daddy, but I can still see him. He blames Robert for the magazine. I know he does.

I can lie and say I bought it or tell the truth and say I stole it. Maybe I should confess. But I don't say anything. I sit silently. If I open my mouth I might just spit blood.

If Momma presses her lips any tighter together, they're going to bust wide open. I'll never be able to convince her that I'm not a sex-crazed sinner. And I haven't even kissed Robert.

Daddy lets go of my chin. Picks the magazine up by its spine and holds it at arm's length as he paces. Momma keeps her distance.

She doesn't need to read the pages, doesn't even have to open the cover to see how terrible they are. She now has absolute proof that her son is gay. And not a repenting, nonpracticing, born-again homosexual—a Sodom-and-Gomorrah, hell-bound, pornography-reading pervert.

My eyes are almost level with the coffee table. Daddy drops the magazine onto it, then stops dead in front of me. He cups his right hand behind my head—a signature move—and presses his left palm against my chest. He is laying hands on the parts of me that are sick, my mind and my soul. Momma gets up from the hearth and puts one hand on top of Daddy's and the other on my forehead. "In the name of Jesus," Daddy prays, "we cast you out."

Hearing my own father talk about me this way is almost more than I can bear. When Jesus cast out demons, they went into pigs that jumped over the cliff and drowned in the sea. How could something so horrible live inside me? Only drunks and cancer patients and men who cheat on their wives get the laying on of hands.

"Yes, Jesus," Momma prays. "Deliver him, Lord." She presses her hands harder into me so the Spirit can flow freely. My chest and skull are going to collapse or explode.

What if I really am possessed by demons? What if Satan disguised his voice so he sounds like God and is deceiving me to think I'm okay? The Bible warns that he comes as a wolf in sheep's clothing. Even the righteous will be deceived. Who am I to think God speaks the truth to me? Maybe I am the pervert they fear. How does anyone know which voice to believe?

My parents' sweaty palms smash into my skin. I used to be as desperate for me to change as they still are. But it doesn't add up. Either God doesn't have the power to change me or He just won't. I know my gayness breaks their hearts, but I'm kind of glad He hasn't changed me. I'm not so sure I want my gayness gone. I'm starting to be okay with it. Is there any way to know for certain that God is?

"Satan," Daddy goes on. "You have no power over our precious child of God." If I'm so precious, why do I need this?

I've heard my father pray with a million sinners at the altar and he's never sounded exactly like this before. I should pray with him, but if something as terrible as the almighty Satan was really in me, I think I'd know it. I think it would be eating me up like acid, from the inside out.

"Heal him, Lord," Momma chimes in.

They echo these same words over and over again. "Heal

him, Lord. Heal him." Faster and faster, louder and louder. Things spin. I am showered with spit. Hands press harder and harder into me. I am wedged tightly between them, but it is as if I watch the whole thing from a distance, from somewhere outside my body. It isn't me they pray for, but some other poor, wretched sinner.

I'm afraid. Scared their prayers won't work; scared they will. But Momma and Daddy are more scared than I am. That's what I hear now, in Daddy's praying: how scared they are. And I know they'll keep praying over me until they get a sign I'm delivered, until I get slain in the Spirit or speak in tongues.

But suddenly Daddy's prayer stops dead in its tracks. Momma follows his lead, takes her hands off me. Is God saying something to them that I can't hear, or was it the doorbell?

Momma and Daddy are out of their trances. They listen.

Cool air rushes to my sweaty skin underneath where Momma's hand was, and I sense what they knew before me. God is with us now just like He was with His disciples in the Upper Room at Pentecost. The Holy Spirit is here in this damp basement den. As thick as the August air on the other side of that tiny basement window. He's not at work changing me, though. I don't feel Him ripping out the sinner by the roots. Did they quit too soon?

God's loving arms are wrapped tight around my shoulders. He has built an invisible shield between me and the prayers of my parents.

Daddy sags like a flat tire. He pushes his glasses up on his nose and kisses me on the forehead. He's all the way on the other side of the den, getting ready to go upstairs, before he turns back and says, "God loves you, son."

Momma kisses my forehead too. Her lips stay pressed tight there for an eternity before pulling back. She brushes the hair away from my face to get a clear view of me. "Vincent," she says. "You know I love you, don't you?"

I do know. And I love her back. But I don't tell her that.

Daddy walks up the steps without another word.

Barehanded now, with no dust rag protecting her, Momma picks up the *First Hand* and carries it to the fireplace. She pulls the metal chain and the wire fireplace screen opens like a drapery. Momma lays the magazine on the metal grate where a neat pile of wood should be stacked. She strikes a foot-long fireplace match and touches its flame to the magazine. She lights the four corners first, then traces along each side. The paper is dry. It catches easily. There is very little blue or green in the flame. Momma blows out the match and drops it in the ash bucket. The magazine burns on, orange and yellow.

Outside I'm calm, but inside I burn with embarrassment, with anger. Angry at Momma and Daddy, at God, Robert, me.

On her way to the stairs, Momma stops by me just long enough to comb her fingers through my hair. I catch her wrist but let go the second I realize what I've done.

The room is calm. Even the magazine has finished burning. But I feel like I've been drowned by a tidal wave and washed out to sea.

I am ashamed and alone. Shaken, shaky. But God is here, the same as He was on the top of the fire tower.

Overhead, footsteps clomp around the kitchen. Cabinet doors open. Dishes bang and clang. Two jumbled voices take turns. It's not over for them either. No matter what the Bible says, how can they believe these horrible things about their only begotten son?

I pull both legs up onto the couch, muddy sneakers and all. I bury my feet under the seat cushion. A smaller triangle of light pours through the window. Dust dances and floats and falls like a summer snow flurry.

The arm of the couch is my headrest. I rub my palms together, back and forth, heating them up with friction. I press the heels of my hands hard against my closed eyelids. Momma's cure for a headache. I don't know if it's the warmth or the pressure that primes the pump, but once the first few tears come, a flood follows.

CHAPTER EIGHT

Clouds cover the moon and all but a few stars. The pitch-black night is a perfect match for the way I feel.

A rectangle of green light glows through Robert's bedroom window. I walk toward it. At least there's no more need for worry about how to wake him up while letting his parents sleep.

The closer I get, the quicker my steps.

After Momma and Daddy laid hands on me, I wept. I slept. I don't know exactly how long, but I woke up on the couch in the dark, a heap of knotted clothes and tangled hair. The smell of smoke brought back the stench of what they did to me.

I didn't go upstairs to wash the dried snot and tears off my face; I just left. Partly I wanted to avoid waking my parents, but mostly I didn't want to let another second tick by before I was with Robert.

I can already tell that their prayers didn't work. Nothing has changed inside me. That doesn't bother me anymore.

I crouch as low as I can when I pass under his parents' windows. I am half prowler, half Romeo.

"Who's out there?" The circular beam of a flashlight lands on the ground in front of me, moves left and then right, like prison guards searching for escaped convicts. The bright light blurs my vision. I can barely see his silhouette in the rectangle of light at the window. "I've got a gun."

I know he does. A .357 Magnum. He taught me how to blast Nehi bottles off a fencepost. "It's me."

"What are you doing out there?" He's happy to see me. It's in his voice.

I stop in the center of the beam. "I couldn't sleep," I say. One day I'll tell him about everything, even the porn. But not tonight. Where would I start?

"Get in here before my dad really does get his gun."

The circle of light follows me as I step toward him. I grab hold of the windowsill to pull myself up. I'm not high enough, so I drop to the ground and try again. Robert's eyes don't move off me as he raises the screen.

On my third attempt Robert says, "Let me help you." He leans out the window. "Put your arms around my neck." As I do, Robert reaches under my armpits, locks his hands behind my back. "One, two ..."

On the count of three, I jump and brace the ball of my bare foot against the brick. Robert straightens at the waist, lifts up, pulls me through his window. My shirt and then my stomach skin catch on something sharp. It hurts, but I don't bother to check for blood. Nothing could pry us apart right now.

Even after I've got both my feet planted on his bedroom floor, Robert doesn't let me go. "What were you doing out there?" With each word he gives my middle a little squeeze, sending little puffs of air out my nose. "You scared me to death." He teases me by trying to put a mad sound in his voice, but he can't pull it off.

I just needed to be with you—that's what I want to say, but those words would sound too corny.

"I'm glad you came," he says.

It's good that the room is lit only by the green glass shade of the reading light that hangs on his headboard—Robert can't see what a mess I am. Actually, it's only my appearance that's a major mess right now. I'm not sure how it happened, but my insides have tidied themselves.

"Ouch." I've been trying to hold it in, but the pain catches up to me.

"Let me see what hurts."

I reach to raise my T-shirt, but Robert beats me to it. I hold my breath while he lifts up the hem. Though the summer night air is warm, it cools the cut. Robert kneels in front of me and puts the flashlight under his chin. The shadows should make him look scary, but they just make him more handsome. In a Count Dracula voice, he says, "Vat have ve here!"

He turns the flashlight back to inspect my wound. With a fingertip softer than Momma's, he draws circles around my cut, kisses the skin just above it, then below. One more kiss on each side.

My lungs huff a gasp of air so loud that he must have heard it. The muscles at the edge of my Levi's quiver, the way Happy does when flies land on her withers.

Robert pulls away. "I'd better go get something for that. Lie down. I'll be right back."

The word *go* echoes in my ears. It's all I can do not to grab him by the wrist and never let him leave.

I lie down and watch him open the door. The hallway light changes the color of the room until he shuts the door behind him. I listen to Robert open and close other doors. I hold my breath while he mumbles with one of his parents. I listen hard, trying to figure out who's saying what, and pray we're not caught. I wonder which one of his parents he's talking to. What are they saying to each other?

If I didn't think they'd hear me, I'd get myself up out of his bed to put on a Barry Manilow record.

Robert comes back through the door carrying hydrogen peroxide, cotton balls, and Merthiolate, all in one hand. In his other hand, a glass of ice water.

He offers me the glass. A few drops of condensation drip onto my chest and soak through my T-shirt. "I thought you might be thirsty."

I lift myself up on my elbows just enough to drink from the glass. A little water leaks from the right corner of my mouth, runs down my chin. With the same finger he used to check my cut, he wipes a drop off my neck.

Robert sets the water and his first-aid kit on the bedside table. He raises my shirt again, over my navel. I arch my back and he pulls it all the way up my chest. He doesn't need my shirt this high just to see the cut. He stares. The silence is deafening.

From the moment I climbed through Robert's window, I could tell there was something new with us. Something more. I don't know if my parents' prayers tore down a wall or built a bridge, but things between Robert and me are somehow different from how they were before, different from how they have ever been between me and any other living soul.

Robert adjusts the green lampshade so a white ray lights up my stomach. He unbuckles my belt and undoes the button of my jeans. My muscle quivers again and he stops—which is good for now.

He soaks a cotton ball in peroxide and presses it into my cut. I raise my head and try to watch the bubbles. When he picks up the Merthiolate, I hold my breath. I hate when my mother uses it. I can feel the burn already. He unscrews the cap and taps the glass wand on the edge of the bottle to shake off the extra drops. He rolls the wand between his fingers and across my cut. It burns worse than I remember. Robert tightens his lips into a small circle, bends closer, and blows a cool stream of air onto my skin. As he moves his lips, this stream passes up and down my cut. When he stops blowing, there is no more pain.

He puts the glass rod back into the bottle and screws the cap on tight. He lines up the Merthiolate beside the peroxide.

"Slide over," he says, pulling the lamp chain. He lies on his side and I turn my head to face him. We are almost close enough to flutter our eyelashes together in a butterfly kiss.

He looks beautiful in this light.

"Let's rub noses like the Eskimosies," I chant like my mother used to.

Robert moves his face even closer to mine. Before I can sing the rest of the rhyme, *And on the count of three let's kiss,* his lips are on mine. They are softer than they have been in any of my million fantasies, softer than Rose Lewis's or the lips of any other girl I've kissed.

He must have brushed his teeth right before bed because he tastes like candy canes. When he breathes out it smells like Christmas.

Robert outlines my lips with his tongue. Clockwise, then counterclockwise. He moves his jaw just enough. Our tongues are in constant motion except for when I stop to feel Robert explore my mouth. His tongue is not hard like Ellen Knight's. Hers felt like a snake trying to poke its way through my cheek.

Like good swimmers, we do not interrupt our swimming to surface for air.

CHAPTER NINE

Momma's Volkswagen is barely able to climb White Oak Mountain. Happy carried Robert and me faster. The speedometer vibrates back and forth so much it's impossible to tell how slow we're really moving. Momma's taking me to Value City to buy clothes for church camp next week.

We weren't going to shop until Momma got her first paycheck, but at breakfast she announced she'd changed her mind. I'm positive she has trapped me in the car to talk about yesterday. She wants to get a read on me and see whether God worked His magic. If she had any idea what happened last night, we wouldn't be driving anywhere.

I woke before sunrise with Robert still curled behind me, one hand over my shoulder, the other under my shirt, his palm cupping my waist. I slid out of his grasp without waking him, but when I sat down on the edge of the bed to tie my shoe, he rolled over and through sleepy puppy-dog eyes said, "When can I see you?" There was desperation in his voice, and I liked it.

I wanted him to say, *Don't go.* But that would be stupid. One of our parents was going to be awake before too long. If they weren't already.

Robert squeezed my waist.

"I don't know," I said, and took his hand. "Sometime today?"

Momma downshifts into second. Robert should be the one driving me to Danville. It should be Robert who helps me pick out my clothes, who watches me turn around in the dressing room mirror and tells me how well things fit.

At breakfast, they didn't mention the magazine, or Robert, or my homosexuality. Maybe there's hope they'll go on believing their prayers were answered, thinking I'm healed.

Even though it's sunny and warm out, the wind is up. It takes both hands for Momma to keep her little car on the road.

An eighteen-wheeler gains on us. I pull out the knob for the hazard light. It blinks red.

"Don't worry. We'll make it," Momma says. She rubs her hand across the dashboard. "Me and this ol' girl climb White Oak Mountain every morning." She puts her hand on the back of my bucket seat and then moves it to my shoulder. I fight the impulse to lean down and pretend my shoe needs tying.

Momma's radio is always tuned in to WVOG, the Voice of God for the People of God. A massive choir sings "How Great Thou Art," Daddy's favorite hymn. He wants me to sing it at his funeral. Momma joins the radio choir. The eighteen-wheeler passes on the left and blows us over. Our front tire drops onto the gravel shoulder. Momma quits singing while she steers us back onto the highway.

The choir sings "A-men" in four-part harmony, and then a preacher's voice comes on the radio. A sermon is the last thing I want to hear, but I don't ask her to change the station. Without my asking she quickly reaches down and turns past the next two religious stations. Then "Copacabana" comes on and she stops.

"Haven't I heard you play this?"

"It's Barry Manilow. I have it on eight-track."

Even though it is clearly not a Christian song, what with all the drinking and dancing and adultery, Momma doesn't change the station. She leans forward and looks through the windshield to the top of the mountain.

I can't help but sing along; I know every word. Momma shakes her shoulders and sways at the waist to the beat of the bongos. If it weren't a sin, I'd swear she was dancing. When we get to the chorus again, she sings along the few words she remembers and makes up the rest. With my eyes and dimples I laugh at her silly lyrics, at the trio we're singing with Barry.

"That must be where you and Robert had your picnic," she says, still seat-dancing.

At least she doesn't call him "that Ingle boy." Momma's gearing up to preach her own sermon. I lean forward and look through the window like she's doing, like I have no idea where we are.

From all the way down here, I see the platform sway with the pine trees. I point and say, "That's where," as if this helps.

"All the way at the top?" The tower bends the same direction as the trees.

"It wasn't this windy the day we rode up there."

"I was going to say," Momma says, leaning back in the driver's seat and setting her eyes on the road again, "it's a wonder you boys didn't get blown off."

I know Momma is trying to break the ice. This is her way of making up for snooping through my room, for not letting us go on and on for eternity pretending I'm not gay. We've got to live in the same house together. At least until I graduate. I know I won't stay mad at her forever.

We don't say more. Barry serenades us with the end of the song, the part where old Lola sits in the disco, thirty years later. She's out of her mind—still in that dress cut down to there—mourning the loss of her one true love, Tony.

Everything around me is the brightest, most perfect version of itself. The greens shimmer in the sun. The black pavement glitters before it disappears under the Volkswagen. The summer wind brings everything to life. Not much could make this drive better. Unless I were in the driver's seat and Robert were beside me. If his hand were under mine while I changed gears, I would not let go until we drove all eighteen miles to Danville. I would put both our lives in danger when I leaned over to kiss him on the ear and neck.

"Poor Lola." Momma's words bring me back inside the car. I was imagining what my pink tissue paper must have looked like from way down here, floating off the fire tower. I wonder what happened to it. "She should have just changed clothes and moved on," she adds.

Momma waits for the song to end before she turns off the radio.

"You know we have to talk about this sometime, Vincent." She doesn't need to clarify what "this" is. I watch myself spin the knob on the door handle to make it clear that now is not the time.

Momma's hands are at ten and two on the steering wheel. Her eyes don't stray from the yellow lines that divide Highway 29.

"We know you know what the Bible says. Your father wants me to make sure there are no doubts that our love for you is unconditional, son. We love you more than our own lives." She moves the hand that was on the two down to my thigh.

"We love you, Vincent," Momma repeats, squeezing my leg. She doesn't release immediately. "But God hates the sin of homosexuality, so we must hate it too, son." She moves her hand back onto the steering wheel, but my leg still feels the pressure. Even though I haven't quit watching my feet, I can tell she has taken her eyes off the road and is staring at my profile.

"And unless God delivered you yesterday, we must pray without ceasing until the day He does," she says, and then turns back toward the pavement.

I'm surprised by her definition of unconditional love. It's not enough. Not nearly enough. How can Momma hate homosexuality and love me?

"Pray your heart out," I say, not even under my breath. I can't believe the words that just jumped out of my own mouth, but I keep going. "The Bible says, 'Ask and it shall be given,' Momma. 'Seek and ye shall find.' But God's got to be bigger than the Bible. Because you and me, we're asking for opposites."

Momma cocks her head and freezes, like a dog watching someone eat steak. She drops her jaw, ready to fight back, but stops herself. I can tell I've got her, so I push more. This time I stare down her profile.

"Don't you think, Mom?"

Value City's parking lot is almost empty when we pull in. Momma parks next to the handicapped space. Rock-star parking.

We walk side by side through the automatic doors. The air in Value City is freezing cold. I stay beside her. Usually I speed off to Menswear, but today we weave together between racks of women's lingerie and shelves of discount shoes, taking our time to get there.

She shops on the opposite side of the rack from me. We move down the aisles flipping and clicking through hangers, running fabric between our fingers. I slide another hanger and unveil a mint-green, plaid western shirt with a solid yolk and pearl buttons. It reminds me of the one Robert wore to ride Happy.

While I hold the hanger, Momma unfastens the pearl snaps and inspects the seams. "Very nicely made," she says. "I couldn't sew it as well myself."

Church camp is in the mountains. It gets cold at night. I'll need something with sleeves.

I check the collar. It's my size. How can a new shirt get a person's heart rate up? I can't look at another thing.

Outside the dressing room, I hand the clothes I need to try on to the lady who's sitting there. It's her job to count items so people don't shoplift. She hands them back to me along with a blue plastic tag that says "4."

Momma walks behind me to the dressing room and pushes open the door. I give her the things I'm not taking in with me, two T-shirts and a pair of sweat pants; I know they'll fit. Momma bows at the waist and motions me through with a wave of her hand. But she doesn't follow me all the way in this time. She pulls the door closed tight. "Let me know if you need help, honey."

I slide the chrome latch closed and lean my back against the door, in case she changes her mind. Finally all alone. I can't believe I said those things and lived. I spoke in my voice, but it wasn't just me talking; it was almost like I was taken over by the Holy Spirit, speaking in tongues. I'm beginning to think Momma might not ever call me on my blasphemy.

"How do they fit?"

I've got the western shirt on now, and it's perfect. I shimmy the overalls past my hips, hold the bib up in front of my chest, and keep it in place with my chin. I can tell they fit without hooking the straps, which are adjustable anyway. I can't wait to see if Robert likes them.

"Vincent?"

I didn't mean to ignore her question. "I'm okay," I blurt. What I mean is that the clothes fit, but a double meaning hits me: For the first time since third grade, I don't feel like there's one thing wrong with me. I *am* okay.

I lean back against the door again, press my feet into the

floor. I bask in fluorescent light and the smell of new clothes. I'm a little afraid to move, to break this peace.

I hand the western shirt and the overalls to Momma. Thank God she hasn't made me try them on in front of her.

Over the top of the door, I see her look at all the clothes I picked out. She reads the price tags but doesn't say anything about them being too expensive. She gets to the western shirt and holds it up in the fluorescent light. She smiles. One by one she fastens the pearl snaps, then folds the shirt. I can't stay mad at her; she's trying so hard.

She's my mother. I love her. There's nothing either of us can do about it.

I slide back the latch—it's like the one on the stalls in the boys' bathroom at school—and I pull the half-door toward me, into the dressing room. Momma takes a step back to make room for me to walk out in my second outfit—corduroy pants and an Oxford shirt. I pose with one hand behind my neck and the other in my back pocket. Momma checks me out top to bottom. I shift into one of the other model poses I've seen in catalogues. I have a million of these. When I was a kid, I used to practice in front of my bedroom mirror.

Like a soldier, I do an about-face, give my rear view. I turn back around again. I have to stand up to her judgment.

She bends down and takes a section of pant leg in hand, rubs her thumb back and forth across it. "Going to get cold up in those mountains," she says and winks, tries to find the right words. "These will keep your legs cozy."

CHAPTER TEN

It is the last night of church camp. Robert couldn't come. He had to help pull tobacco.

The tallest of the campfire flames are Pastor Neff's height. Teenagers sit hip to hip on a circle of telephone pole benches. All our eyes are swollen from staying up hours past lights-out every night this week. The heat from the fire makes everyone's cheeks rosy.

Here I sit. A homosexual. Since I was at church camp last year, I've made out with Robert three times. As soon as I get off this mountain, I know I'll do it again.

Every single moment of this week was designed to scare us teenagers so bad we repent and come back to Jesus. Most years this works on me, but this time it didn't. The Bible classes and the sermons have been painless.

At the end of every service, Pastor Neff tries to get us down at the altar confessing. Not even one little tug at my heart all week. When Pastor Neff says search deep, I do, but I don't find anything that I need to leave at the altar. I guess God isn't just bigger than church. He's bigger than church camp, too.

There are campfires every night of church camp, marshmallow roasts and stupid skits. It's the part of camp every kid looks forward to. There's just something about flames that we love.

Tonight there is a wooden cross planted at the edge of the fire ring—a two-by-four nailed to a fencepost. It's our last night; they say it's our final chance to get right with the Lord before they send us back home to our parents. Every other year, I have been the first person confessing and repenting. But tonight, no matter what the Bible says, I know things between God and me are okay.

Pastor Neff made the cross himself. I saw him this morning after breakfast, hammering behind the tabernacle.

As we sat down, Pastor Neff gave us each a little white square of paper and a miniature-golf pencil. Now he raises his hands toward the starless sky and explains that we are to write down our biggest sin on the paper. He tells us to pray and ask God to reveal which sin to write. It should be the one we can't get control over, the one that keeps us farthest from God.

Since the moment I quit trying to control my homosexuality, God has never left my side.

The log benches are too close to the fire, but they're held in place with railroad stakes, so we're stuck where our eyelashes singe and jeans melt to our skin. It reminds me of what hell will be like. I bet the pastor did that on purpose.

Pastor Neff hasn't said so yet, but we're going to nail these papers with our sins written on them to the cross. After we do that, we're going to torch the whole thing. There's a can of lighter fluid at the foot of the cross.

All this drama is designed to break us down. Usually it works on me, but this year I'm numb to it. I read my pencil. PIRATE'S COVE PUTT-PUTT. We went there on a youth outing. I got a hole in one.

Stephanie Neff strums the song "Pass It On." The words are *It only takes a spark to get a fire going*. It's just a little bit too obvious. Stephanie scans the circle, makes eye contact with any poor sinner who will look back.

Before Momma and Daddy laid hands on me, I wouldn't have had to think twice about it. I would have written *Homosexuality* on my paper and been one of the first to finish. But tonight, I have to rack my brain. If I'm not begging God to deliver me from being gay anymore, what else is there?

We all know the words to "Pass It On," but only a few people sing along, and they're just mumbling under their breath. Most kids stare at their slip of paper, roll their putt-putt pencils between their fingers. Sheri Shields flattens her paper on her knee and cups her hands around the words she writes. She looks like she's guarding test answers from a cheater. A few kids know just what to write and finish quickly. They wear nervous smiles and fold their papers once, twice—as tight as they can make it and still be able to hammer a nail through. Ian Altham told me at dinner that he brought four joints in his pack of Marlboro Reds. I wonder if he's writing that.

Pastor Neff sees that Laurie Orange is through writing and leads her by the elbow up to the cross. He takes a nail from the egg basket that dangles on his forearm and hands it to her, then the hammer. Laurie's first whack shakes the cross. Jeff Neff, Pastor Neff's son, has to come up behind it and brace the cross. He stands with his shoulder against the fencepost, like a football player shoving slides across the field during practice. One by one people take their turn with the hammer. The sound echoes across the mountain. Very soon the cross is covered in white. It blooms. We should have used red paper.

Laurie Orange's brother Lenny has his turn. His paper is folded too small. It's too thick to drive a nail through. He has to unfold it.

We should be roasting marshmallows over this campfire. Anything but this. I'll have to take my turn sooner or later. All eyes will be on me. Everyone here knows what I should write. Just like we all know Ian Altham should write *Smoking pot.*

I know what the rest of the world would tell me to write, but my hand doesn't move. I can only read my pencil over and over again.

Somehow I can't bring myself to do it. I used to think God would save me from my homosexuality, but after the laying on of hands, after spending the night in Robert's bed and almost every day of that week with him, I realize God did hear me pray to be delivered. He didn't answer the way I thought he would, but He did answer.

Now that I've loved and kissed Robert, I'm pretty sure the biggest thing wrong with being gay is that the Bible says it's wrong. The way I see it, there are many things worse than what Robert and I feel for each other, what we do.

If I am such a sinner, why hasn't God turned tail and run? I feel Him as close now as I ever have. I've always felt Him. There with Robert and me on the top of the fire tower. He was with me when I cut my stomach climbing through the window. He didn't disappear when we kissed.

More people finish writing and nail their sins to Pastor Neff's cross. I keep listening, but God still hasn't revealed my sin.

Writing *Homosexuality* would be like saying there is evil in what Robert and I do. And I won't do that to Robert, even if it means treading water in the lake of fire for eternity.

I know what's written in the Bible and what my Daddy preaches about homosexuality. All have sinned. I have many sins. But in this moment, I know beyond a shadow of a doubt that being gay is not one of them. I may die and go to hell one day, but it won't be because I love Robert.

Now Stephanie plays "Fire and Rain." She's picking instead of strumming. Her playing sounds like a piano, one note at a time. I like it. "Fire and Rain" is not even a church song. It's about suicide. If Pastor Neff knew that, he'd make Stephanie stop playing it. According to the Bible, suicide is one of the few sins worse than homosexuality. You're dead, so you can't be forgiven for it.

Only two of us still have to nail our sins to the cross. The other person is Julie Taylor. She's such a goody-goody she's probably having trouble coming up with a sin. Pastor Neff watches us. He wants us to write now. If we don't finish soon, he is going to come help us.

I keep the pencil lead from actually touching the page. I mime-write a row of tall loops, the way Miss Cummings made us do in third grade to learn cursive. I start to draw the wing of a cardinal, a simple sketch like Momma used to make on the back of her church bulletin when she was trying to keep me from getting restless during Daddy's long sermons.

The campfire has started to die down, but no one will dare interrupt this moment to throw more wood on it. The added darkness is a welcome thing.

Pastor Neff nods in my direction. It's my turn. Now or never. I stand up and walk behind the circle of teenagers, carry my paper to the cross. Pastor Neff takes me by the elbow and leads me the last few steps. He hands me the hammer. There was a time when I thought if I pounded myself in the chest with a hammer I could beat the queer out of me.

I find a bare spot of wood on an arm of the cross. The wood is soft. My slip of paper is damp from the wet night air. It is easy to drive the nail through.

Once Julie has nailed her sin, Pastor Neff squeezes a stream of lighter fluid onto the cross. He soaks the sins in it, then strikes a match. He touches it to the first paper that Laurie Orange nailed on. It catches faster than my magazine did. Fire spreads quickly from one paper to the other. It climbs up the fencepost and out each arm of the cross until the whole thing is in flames. My cheeks burn. The rubber toes of my sneakers scorch my feet. Fire crackles. I can't hear the guitar anymore. My cardinal turns to ashes.

God's voice comes in so loud and clear that I am surprised the others in the circle don't turn around and look to see who is speaking.

"The reason I never changed you, Vincent," God says to only me, "is that I love you the way you are, the way I created you." I've been feeling this recently, knowing it's true, but it's the first time these words have passed from God's lips to my ears. My heart leaps higher than the tallest campfire flame, leaps up to God.

Tears had been trickling, but now they flood. Again the darkness of this night is welcome.

Kris Thompson, Stephanie's boyfriend, puts his arm around her shoulder, which makes her mess up a chord change. He kisses the crown of her head, right where her hair parts.

This time tomorrow, I'll be kissing Robert.